LEARNING TO SPELL

Lynn Ericson

ISBN-13: 978-1-7355525-6-9

Library of Congress Control Number: 2021914748

LOST IN THE WOOD PRESS

www.lostinthewoodpress.com

Conway, Arkansas, U.S.A.

Dedication

This book is gratefully dedicated to all the English and Writing teachers and mentors who encouraged me, helped me grow, and taught me the importance of respecting the Narrative.

ACKNOWLEDGEMENTS

Cover Design by Peter O'Connor
https://bespokebookcovers.com

Copy Editing by Elise Williams Rikard
https://www.elisewilliamsrikard.com

Editorial Assistance provided by
Fellowship of Conway Literati

CHAPTER ONE
Come Up and See Me

Sylvie's long-anticipated letter of acceptance into the Lovelace Community College of Applied Magic did not arrive by the traditional method of a bespectacled messenger mouse wearing a green waistcoat and gold-buckled shoes. It arrived in the form of an elegant, dark-skinned woman slipping Sylvie a business card with her hotel room number on the back.

The moment instantly triggered an indecipherable rush of emotions. For starters, the woman was Diana Taylor—*the* Diana Taylor, whose portrayal of Lark Starling had breathed life into everyone's favorite apprentice enchantress in the *Lovelace* movies. Sylvie had had the biggest girl crush on Lark Starling since her early teens, and on Diana by extension, but it was *just* a girl crush. At least she was pretty sure it was just a girl crush. There had been just enough doubt in Sylvie's mind to have been briefly curious if she was bi-curious when the fan magazines announced Diana had come out as bi-sexual, but that thought had quickly been buried and forgotten in Sylvie's graveyard of irrelevant musings.

Now suddenly here was Sylvie's childhood hero inviting her up to her hotel room after the convention closed down for the night. Sylvie figured that gave her two seconds tops to decide just how totally straight she was. Then Diana let her off the hook with a quiet, apologetic chuckle.

"Ookay. That sounded less seedy in my head," Diana said. "I just have a big personal favor to ask, I'll feel better knowing all the paparazzi are on the other side of a locked door, and I won't get a break from the convention until my nine o'clock panel is over. Come find me?"

Sylvie blinked. "What sort of favor?"

"Personal," Diana repeated.

Sylvie considered protesting that they'd only just met an hour ago when she'd picked Diana up at McCarran International. She'd worked hard to make sure she'd be the convention volunteer to get that particular assignment, but an hour's acquaintance seemed pretty shaky ground on which to plant a top-secret personal favor.

Diana caught Sylvie's eye sternly before she decided whether to let the protest out. "Pretend for just one moment," Diana said, "that I was a mysterious mouse in a green waistcoat and think how hard you'd be kicking yourself tomorrow for walking away from the invitation."

She plucked the business card back out of Sylvie's unresisting fingers and gracefully flipped it around to display the hand-printed room number—511—six inches from Sylvie's face. "Show up and there will be adventure. Walk away and I'll give the adventure to someone else." She flipped the business card through her fingers again and wedged the end gently between Sylvie's lips. "I'll see you at ten fifteen." She gave Sylvie a final, friendly smile, spun on her heels, and strolled off toward the elevators, dragging her suitcase behind her.

"Well, that explains a few things." A hand reached out to pluck the card from Sylvie's mouth before she quite realized she hadn't done it herself yet. "Her room number and everything? I'd dump me too if I had Lark Starling on the hook."

"I don't have anyone 'on the hook,'" Sylvie said tersely as she snatched the card back out of Brian's hand, "much less another woman. And I never dumped you. We went out a few times. You failed the roller coaster test. End of story." Beneath what might have been either an honest attempt to grow a beard or just a week's worth of stubble, the lanky young man was cute enough; but if cute was all she'd wanted, Sylvie wouldn't have gone looking past the home-town crowd she'd left behind.

"Tests aren't cool," Brian said. "And call it what you want, the old 'business card between the lips with her room number on it' trick is some heavy-duty flirting. I saw it in a movie somewhere. Diana Taylor wants you bad, girl."

"She needs a favor," Sylvie said with a scowl.

"A favor with your lipstick on it." Brian grinned.

"I'm not wearing lipstick." Sylvie sighed, rolling her eyes. "And tests are what dating is all about. You passed a lot of them. You're a good guy, Brian. You're just not *my* good guy. Now let it drop while you're still a good guy."

"You could have us both," Brian offered. "Me and her? I won't mind—especially not if your hot movie star friend is up for a threesome. She likes guys, too, you know." There was just enough sparkle in his eyes for Sylvie to brush it off as a forgivable—if transparent—fishing expedition.

"Tell you what," Sylvie offered. "I've never been with a woman, but if Diana Taylor seduces me you'll be the first to know."

"Seriously?" Brian asked.

"No." She gave him a gentle shove. "Now go. Aren't you supposed to be helping set up the art show or the dealer's room or something?"

"No to which part?" He laughed.

"All of it!" She thrust a finger pointedly off toward the conference rooms. "Go!"

He finally went, but not without giving her one last suggestive grin.

Sylvie sighed again, tucked the card away, and headed for the communal convention suite where, as a volunteer, she'd stowed her gear. A room of her own for the weekend was an expense she didn't need, and she expected sleep to be in short supply anyway. It always was at a fantasy convention. Any sleep she did grab would be in the limo she'd brought Diana and the other V.I.P.s in from the airport with. It wouldn't be the first or last time she did that. The car she drove every day for work had become something of a second home, and she had it free and clear for the weekend. Her boss's daughter was a huge Lark Starling fan, and Sylvie had been able to sweet talk him into loaning the limo to the convention for the weekend upon the promise his girl would get to meet Diana.

Diana had been the last of the guests Sylvie had needed to pick up. Her only big obligation left as a volunteer would be to help with the costume contest, and that wouldn't be until tomorrow evening. That freed her up now to hit the convention floor and have some fun. Step one would be getting into her own costume. Costuming had been Mom's big thing and Sylvie had inherited the bug. She'd gone to conventions off and on her entire life and couldn't recall ever attending one without spending most of it in costume. She'd very nearly gone with a *Lovelace* costume in Diana's honor this time, but Manami—her roommate and partner in cosplay crime—had assured her that would come across as desperate fangirl and instead convinced Sylvie to join her in a steampunk look for the weekend.

Now Sylvie was happy she had. She'd have been even happier if her corset showed a bit less cleavage and maybe if the costume had a few more inches worth of skirt—like twelve or fifteen. To be honest, though, she'd been a teenager the last time she'd owned a costume that *hadn't* been designed to get as many guys staring at her as possible. Even at mundane parties she dressed to attract attention. That was sort of the point, wasn't it? Going to a party to be overlooked and ignored was like going to the theater to read a book. The convention setting was just an invitation to get creative and artistic about attracting attention.

Sylvie was pleased to see a nice little queue had formed at the registration desk despite the early hour. The Fantasy Convention with No Name—a.k.a. NoNaCon—was neither old nor prestigious but had established itself as an important part of the local fan community with hopes that attendance would surpass a thousand for the first time this year. Much of that hope was pinned on the fact they'd managed to book Diana as guest of honor. That had been a major coup given the size and budget of the convention. In previous years it was all they could manage to book an author with some national name recognition or the actor behind a recurring minor character on a TV show long past its glory days.

Yes, it had been a few years since the last of the *Lovelace* films, but Diana remained an A-list convention guest anywhere in the country—and possibly anywhere in the world. Unlike her co-stars, Diana hadn't gone on to make any other films since, but she'd developed a reputation as "the approachable one". She did things like quietly attend conventions in costume and incognito until the last day, when she'd sign stuff for the people she'd had fun with before heading out—or she'd host room parties and invite random attendees, or hold a charity raffle for seats at a role-playing game session where she'd serve as game master. The larger world of pop-culture might have started to lose interest in Diana Taylor, but serious fantasy fans had never flagged in their enthusiasm for her.

So would it be so bad if Diana really was hitting on her, Sylvie wondered? Sylvie dressed for conventions knowing guys would hit on her probably a dozen or more times over the course of a weekend. She could show up to a convention dressed for Sunday school and they'd probably *still* hit on her half a dozen times. If she wasn't going to let that discourage her, then surely she could live with being the girl who turned down a night with Diana Taylor. So, no, it wasn't bad if Diana had been flirting with her. What would be bad would be becoming the girl who turned down a night with Diana Taylor and then spent her life wishing she hadn't. No pressure, though. She had several whole hours—going from a cold start—to get it straight in her own head how she felt about kissing another woman. With any luck, whichever direction that went, the rest would follow.

And then it dawned on Sylvie she'd already decided to meet Diana at her room. How could she not? Brian was probably wrong anyway. He had a rather mediocre track record at getting inside women's heads. Plus, even if Diana had been flirting, it was a distressingly "guy" attitude to just assume that seduction would follow.

Sylvie had made it into the bathroom of the con suite with her costume—and most of the way into the Victorianish outfit of lace and leather and buckles and gears—before she decided that any consternation she might be feeling over the whole matter of Diana wasn't even hers. It was the ingrained and often unwelcome morality of the small town she'd been trying so hard to leave behind. She wasn't staring into the mirror trying to decide if she wanted to kiss Diana Taylor. She was staring into the mirror trying to decide if wanting to kiss Diana would make her a bad person. The fact of the matter was, right here, right now, she neither wanted to kiss Diana nor was repulsed by the thought of kissing Diana. If Diana wanted to seduce her it was up to Diana to make the sales pitch—just like it would be with any guy she felt ambivalent about. All that mattered was that she felt safe about going to Diana's room and that she had now given herself permission to do whatever the heck she wound up wanting. Conventions were for adventures. *Life* was for adventures.

"Knock knock! Are you decent?" Manami didn't wait for an answer before barging in. Manami never did. That had been one of the first things Sylvie had learned about rooming with a "lady of burlesque"—or at least about rooming with this one. As a stripper at The Rabbit Hole, Manami had developed a very cavalier attitude about other women's state of undress. Or maybe she'd always been that way. At any rate, the world was Nami's locker room and all the women simply team mates. Sylvie had gotten used to it soon enough. At the moment she was mostly into costume anyway. Sylvie adjusted her bowler hat in the mirror as Manami closed the door behind her and dumped her own cosplay gear onto an empty corner of the bathroom counter.

"Looking good," Manami said, giving Sylvie the once-over before she began slipping out of her street clothes. Her Japanese name, Japanese features, and Japanese birth aside, Nami was a local girl with a local accent. Her family had immigrated when she was a baby and they'd settled in Vegas. "Are we on for the eight-o'clock Lovelace panel?" she asked.

"Of course," Sylvie said as she began buckling on the leather belts and straps that held her steampunk arsenal of gadgets—a mix of functional tools and purely decorative ones. "Was it wishful thinking or did I see Martin Kight here too?"

Manami cocked an alarmed eyebrow as she began securing a black lace corset on over the red cotton shift she'd already been wearing under her street clothes. "I *hope* not. I'm pretty sure he and Diana still aren't on speaking terms."

Sylvie nodded. The two actors had had a highly publicized falling out a couple of years after the last of the *Lovelace* films wrapped, and it had been tabloid fodder ever since. That never stopped fans from hoping for their reconciliation for a reunion movie. "I guess it's too much to hope he saw her on the guest list and showed up to make amends?" Fair or not, everyone blamed Martin rather than Diana. Martin had always been the cast's bad boy, and Diana was everyone's darling.

"Doesn't hurt to dream," Nami said.

"Speaking of, Diana actually invited me up to her room tonight. Want to be my plus one?" Sylvie asked.

Nami looked at her askance. "Did Diana *say* she was up for a threesome?"

Sylvie retaliated with an obligatory swat on the shoulder. "Not you too." Sylvie sighed. "Not helpful. She said she needed a favor."

"I don't know which part of all that to disbelieve first." Nami smirked.

"Fine. Don't come." Sylvie rolled her eyes. "Just don't come crying to me that you passed up an evening with Lark Starling."

"Sorry." Nami smiled apologetically. "But if she's asking you for a favor in private it's probably...private. Thanks—it's tempting—but unless she really invited you to bring someone, I'm sure I won't be welcome no matter what's up."

"Momma always warned me you burlesque girls were sticklers for etiquette." Sylvie sighed.

"The stereotype's gotta come from somewhere," Nami said.

Once they were both properly costumed to look like mashups of a mad scientist, a Victorian lady, and a lingerie model, they went to browse the dealer room, where Nami insisted on buying Sylvie a little stuffed dragon that could perch neatly on her steam-punk bowler hat. Then it was off to join their scheduled game session of Labyrinths & Legerdemain. A couple of times during the evening Sylvie flashed a fake engagement ring at guys whose approach displayed a miserable lack of empathy. She also discretely pocketed the ring once to flirt with a much more promising guy she let recruit her for a live-action role-playing session the next day.

Sylvie and Manami arrived early enough to the eight-o'clock *Lovelace* panel to get decent seats. It turned out that Diana *was* joined unannounced by one of her co-stars—but it was Felicity Ward, not Martin Kight. The surprise appearance of the angel-faced blond actress, who'd portrayed Lark's best friend, Holly Marsh, was met with enthusiastic applause from the standing-room-only crowd—even if it didn't qualify as a "we're getting the band back together" moment. The two of them were joined in the panel by a well-known author of *Lovelace* fan fiction, by a UNLV professor who taught a literature course on the original *Lovelace* novels and their impact on society, and by a writer for a popular online game that totally wasn't inspired by the *Lovelace* universe, honest.

The panel was billed as a discussion of the lasting impact of the stories on pop-culture, but the actual substance didn't turn out to be overly substantial. It was mostly a chance to listen to amusing nostalgic anecdotes that carried an occasional hint of scandal from people connected with the milieu, while some attempts were made—mostly by Professor Warren Hawkes—to link them forward to current phenomena in pop culture. The discussion wasn't novel, and it wasn't deep, but it was a fun excuse to bask in the presence of a couple of beloved actors. It wasn't until the question-and-answer portion at the end when the inevitable question about further movies came up that things went a bit off script.

"I'm not against it," Felicity said. "*Lovelace* has been good to me, and I had a lot of fun playing Holly. But the more I think about it the more I believe the modern franchises are getting it right. They're hammering out the idea that it's about the world, not the characters. Back when the characters were just words on a page or pictures in a comic book, they could be timeless. The kids were kids for twenty years or more. Adults would stay frozen at the same age while whole generations came and went in the real world. People had their imaginary friends that never went away and hardly ever changed. Today, we can make our imaginary friends more real than ever—but it turns out that comes at a price. Fans still want me to be Holly for them, but they'd never accept me as teenage Holly anymore. How much longer would you even accept me as undergrad Holly? I'm already closer to 30 than 20. I age. So either Holly ages too, or someone has to go out and find a new Holly. Oh, sure, we're starting to see actors de-aged on film and even performing after their deaths, but it's still just an expensive gimmick.

"So we've got this fight between people wanting pristine continuity in the portrayal of their favorite characters by a single actor versus people's desire to keep their favorite characters trapped in amber, dependable and unchanging—which can't be done without changing out actors. Historically, most film franchises have just done a clean-break and started over every time they had to recast, which is why we have so many reboots. Sometimes the reboots are better than the original, honestly, but that doesn't stop old fans from feeling they've lost old friends when the continuity goes away.

"The move to focusing on worlds over individual characters gets around that by letting us fall in love with ensembles. When the demands of reality rip a favorite character out of the story by removing the actor, studios leave themselves a new option beyond re-casting, rebooting, and dropping the setting. What I'm trying to say is I'm comfortable thinking that Holly's story has been told but that *Lovelace* should be bigger than me or her or any of us. I think it's more likely that if I show up in any future films it'll be in a supporting role, or even as a cameo, and I'm okay with that."

"All of which fits neatly," Diana said, "with what I've been saying since Arthur dropped off the grid. Celebrity comes at a price he can't or isn't willing to pay anymore. For me, Arthur is Isaac and always will be. I can't imagine playing across from anyone else any more than I can imagine continuing Lark's story without Isaac. I'm not up for one of those depressing, 'We grew apart,' or, 'He suffered a brain aneurysm off screen,' explanations for writing him out of the story. Lark and Isaac are off living their happily ever after. That truth about my own imaginary friends is very important to *me* as a fan so you'll never see me playing Lark again as anything more than a cameo. That would be true even if I still saw myself in an acting career.

"But the point I haven't spoken up about before is I don't want anyone else to consider my take on what's happening with Lark and Isaac to be any sort of official canon." Diana turned to the fan-fiction author. "Helen, some of your most popular stories ship me with Felicity here, don't they? Lark with Holly I mean."

"All of them, actually," Helen agreed. "I write them all on a single timeline."

"And I think that's great," Diana said encouragingly. "You've basically developed your own canon to bring continuity into your own timeline. It's the idea that there's one single inviolable set of facts about Lark that worries me because Lark *has* no facts. She isn't real. Well, okay, I'd argue she *is* real, but not like you or me. Fictional creatures are fractal creatures. The very act of sharing them shatters them into divergent realities. My Lark Starling is who *I* need her to be. Your Lark Starling," Diana said, pointing to Helen, "is who *you* need her to be. Her Lark Starling is who *she* needs her to be." At this last Diana pointed out into the audience as if at random, but it was Sylvie she singled out and whose eye she caught in the process. "Our imaginary friends are very important, but we shed too many tears and share too many poison words over a false premise that they can have some sort of independent reality just because they leapt into our minds from the same book or movie screen and continue to share a name.

"I don't own Lark. I own *my* Lark. Helen's Lark Starling could go off and sleep with the entire cast of *What's Wrong with Rhonda* and it wouldn't pose a moment's threat to the integrity of *my* imaginary friend because they're entirely different people. I'll just put down Helen's book if I don't like what I'm seeing. I don't have to accept it as part of my Lark's story. I can't and I won't participate in another *Lovelace* movie to any meaningful degree but please don't let me be the reason anyone holds back from sharing their own versions of *Lovelace*. Let the sequels roll. Don't wait on me. And if anyone ever does re-cast Lark Starling, please don't invoke my name as some sort of curse against them. We always rewrite and re-imagine our heroes. We always have. We're supposed to."

As they were leaving the conference room, funneling out past the people waiting to funnel in, they nearly collided with Brian as he fought to make his way through the crowded hall. "Sylvie! Yes!" He exclaimed. "Got time for a quick favor?"

"Maybe. What favor are you offering?" Sylvie grinned.

"Ha ha. I left the flash drive with my presentation up in the Davis room and my panel starts in two minutes," Brian said. "Can you do your thing and meet me with it in Foxx? I'll owe you another one."

"Oooh. Are you asking for her R-rated thing or her triple-X thing?" Nami asked playfully. "They're both good."

"Her hurrying thing." Brian glared.

"Sure." Sylvie sighed, but it was for form's sake. It was always nice to have an excuse. "The flash drive that looks like a sword?"

"Yes! On the key chain." Brian clapped his hands together prayerfully in a quick gesture of thanks and then reversed direction back the way he'd come.

"You got this?" Nami asked. "I've got my own places to be."

"I've got this." Sylvie nodded. "Just hold my dragon." She tipped her bowler off, dragon and all, into Manami's hands so quickly that Nami almost fumbled them. "Go on. I'll get her back later."

Without further delay, Sylvie started hustling off through the crowd, dodging aliens and superheroes and steampunk robots until she broke into the relative clear of the main hall. It was a good main hall. She liked it. They might as well have laid it out just for her. She already had her route mapped out in her head before she stepped into it. A four-foot wall ran around the perimeter of the room, setting off the outer walkway from the inner lounge area. Normally that allowed unobstructed traffic flow around the outer wall, but now, for the convention, the outer walkway was lined with autograph tables that narrowed the channel—even though it was too late in the day for anyone to be manning them. Combine that with the fact that this was a peak traffic moment between sessions, with all the attendees suddenly hurrying into and out of conference rooms, off to find snacks and restrooms, or crushing into the central lounge area in search of the table their next game would be hosted at, and the open area had turned into an obstacle course. Cool.

Three steps took Sylvie up to the low wall, where she mounted it so smoothly it was fair to say she glided onto it rather than climbing. Then she was on her feet, pacing briskly and sure-footedly down the six-inch-wide span like it was her own private highway through the crowd. It actually worked to her advantage that some of the people stopped and gawked at her like she was a performer, so that when she reached a gap in the wall she didn't have to guess where everyone would be moving. She just dropped off into a hole in the crowd, wiggled through, and glided smoothly back up onto the wall at the far side without missing a step.

There was a lot of steampunk couture out there that would have made the trick difficult, but Sylvie never put up with that sort of nonsense in her costumes. High-heeled boots were right out. She always stuck to soft, sensible, and supple leather that let her put her foot down properly and feel the solid ground supporting every step. Her one concession to style was allowing the boots a ridiculous number of buckles. She also avoided what she thought of as "mullet skirts"—with the mini-length front and the flowing train behind—and went all in on the buckled leather miniskirt, slit for freedom of movement and with brief bike shorts beneath. She wasn't about to let etiquette or a floor costume hobble her.

Toward the end of the hall a permanent decorative canopy had been erected over the lounge area. Its supporting posts offered good handholds, and she knew from experience they'd bear her weight. She scrambled easily up one to grab a stout cable that secured it to the second-floor balcony, then she swung hand-over-hand until she'd reached the railing. On the final swing she had enough momentum to grab the top of the railing with one hand, then to rotate so she was clinging to it with both. Kicking off from the lower edge of the balcony enabled her to push her weight up onto her arms, throw her chest onto the railing, then lift it enough to get a knee under her. In a moment, she had rolled over and onto the balcony, where she paused for a theatrical little spread-armed bow to the crowd below, which had gone from gawking to applauding. It was nice having an audience. It might even make the talking to she'd likely be getting from hotel security worth it.

There was no time to bask in applause, though, and it could only increase her risk of getting in trouble with the hotel, so Sylvie pushed her way into the Davis conference room. "Mel! Flash drive!" She held up her cupped hands as she called to the man who was fiddling with the projector at the front of the room. He picked up the tiny toy sword and cocked a questioning eyebrow back at her. She nodded. He threw. She had to leap to intercept the drive. It bobbled off her fingertips once, but she managed to catch it before it hit the floor. With a quick salute of thanks, she was gone.

Dropping down to grab the cable would have been riskier than swinging up from it, so instead of reversing her original route Sylvie headed for the nearby stairs. Halfway down to the first landing, she bypassed another traffic jam by slipping over the rail and lowering herself down its supporting grill until her feet touched the next railing down. Then she spun about, crouched down, and basically repeated the process until she had just a short drop to a clear space at the bottom. Landing lightly, she hustled back into the main room, repeated her waltz along the low wall, and wound up near the corner across from where Brian had bumped into her. Pushing her way into the room there, she called out a quick heads-up and tossed the key chain across the room in a graceful arc that was noticeably more on-target than Mel's throw had been. Brian caught it easily and mouthed a quiet, "You're awesome!" to her before she darted off for the costuming panel, which would be her final scheduled stop for the evening before her date with Diana. She was still getting applause as she hurried away.

"Entertainer or Olympian?" the woman beside her on the panel asked as Sylvie slid into her chair. Clearly, the woman had been out there recently enough to see much of Sylvie's parkour display.

"I hope not!" Sylvie laughed. "Though I hear the Olympic committee really wants to add in parkour, and my roommate keeps trying to lure me onto the stage with her. She says we should do a rabbit-and-magician act." Sylvie knew that statement begged further explanation, but the panel was called to begin—so she simply let it hang.

CHAPTER TWO
An Attic Out of Place

Sylvie found herself standing outside room five eleven of the Royal Arc Hotel at precisely ten seventeen, braced for whatever lay beyond it that might constitute an adventure. She hadn't caught up with Nami yet so was still missing both dragon and bowler—but that was okay, right? Of course it was. She was here as a favor; not for costume judging. She stared at the closed door for a bit and realized she was fidgeting with the fake engagement ring. She started to pull it off, wondered why, slid it back on, hesitated, pulled it off, then finally slid it into a pouch on her belt. She knocked. She waited. She knocked. She waited. A middle-aged couple in matching blue *Interstellar 2000* uniforms wandered by loaded down with merchandise from the dealer room.

Sylvie knocked again louder. She let out a long, heavy breath. She rolled her eyes. A quote about never meeting one's idols flitted across her mind. She checked the time on the deceptively antique-looking pocket watch that hung from a fob attached to her leather corset. Though it was primarily there for costume, she always tried to keep the watch accurate so she didn't have to break character in order to check the time on her phone. Not quite twenty past the hour yet. Maybe Diana's phone wasn't in sync with Sylvie's watch? Maybe she got held up in that last panel or waylaid by fans? If Diana had been just a friend she was meeting, how late would Sylvie have let her be before giving up? Ten minutes? Maybe fifteen. Yeah. Fifteen tops.

No one else was waiting on Sylvie. The convention was in shutdown mode, with only a few semi-official events and unofficial room parties still going on for the die-hard attendees. She could cut Diana a little slack before admitting she'd been stood up.

Sylvie slumped down against the wall across from Diana's door, pulled out her phone, and busied herself with searching the internet for steampunk-themed phone cases so that next time maybe killing time wouldn't clash with her costume aesthetic. Patience, she reflected as the minutes ticked by, was not her favorite virtue.

A group of young men—not costumers, but still convention-goers from their name badges—wandered by talking among themselves. Even without looking up from her phone, Sylvie could feel their eyes on her as they took advantage of their elevation to look down her intentionally revealing corset. If she tried she was sure she could catch some of them staring at her legs too, lamenting that she'd folded them carefully when she sat down—or perhaps trying to will her short skirt just a little shorter. She didn't mind. She quite liked it as long as they didn't get rude. Someone always did eventually, of course. That was one of the most mystifying things about men. Not all men, of course, or there'd be no point in playing the game with them at all, but too many wanted everything or nothing. Men practically always wanted to look, but show a little bit of flesh and the more lamentable of them took it as a promise you were down for the whole mating dance, complete with consummation.

That was part of why she loved the steampunk look, though. Doctor up most any defensive device with a few fake gears and a little bronze paint, and she could blend it right into her costume. Right now she was openly wearing pepper spray, an actual police baton, an amazingly loud whistle, and a fully functional electroshock wand, all of them out where she could reach them at a moment's notice. No one had batted an eye about any of it all day. The fan life was awesome on so many levels. Of all that gear, she'd only ever used the pepper spray in earnest and only once—but as the only child of a slightly paranoid small-town police officer, she knew how to use all of it. She'd even learned how to shoot a gun and had participated in a couple of county-level martial arts tournaments before her dad was satisfied. Good at any of it? No. But good enough to get the average creep considering that just maybe "no" means "no."

One of the guys complimented Sylvie on her costume as he thrust a flier down at her. It advertised a room party. He was cute and made a decent first impression as he invited her to join. She begged off but held onto the flier and was serious when she told him she might check it out if the friend she was waiting on flaked out on her. She'd refrained from making any other plans because of Diana, and it was still awfully early to just crawl off to a broken night's sleep in the limo. The guys moved on. She checked the time and found she'd been sitting there for more than ten minutes now. It was nearly half past ten. She sighed and stared at the door, trying to will Diana to open it, to peer out, and to apologize for being in the shower. That didn't seem to work any better than the guys willing her skirt up. Her eyes did fall on a little corner of plastic peeking out from under the door though. A room key? A credit card?

Sylvie scooted across the hall and tugged at the plastic until it edged its way out into the open. It was a room key. Was it Diana's? Was it a gift from a caller hoping to lure Diana into some other bed for the night? She flipped the card over and back, looking for a room number, finding none. She'd at least need to turn this in to the hotel desk. No one with acceptable motives would want to risk a coded and active room key floating around the hotel. Maybe this was the whole reason Diana was a no-show. Maybe she'd dropped the key card on her way out of the room and was right now either trying to retrace her steps or to convince some overzealous clerk who'd never seen a *Lovelace* movie that she was the real Diana Taylor.

Feeling a little better for having a reasonable explanation for why she'd been stood up, Sylvie got up and tried one more time knocking loudly at the door. When there was still no answer, she tried the key on the door. The door balked at her first attempt but lit up green at the second. A little beep and a whir announced that the lock had been disengaged.

"Hello? Diana?" Sylvie called, peering into the dark room beyond the door. It smelled of incense. Soft instrumental music with a meditative Asian sound floated out of the darkness. "Are you here? You dropped your room key." No one answered. The light from the hallway fell on an overturned chair, an open folder, and a scattering of papers on the carpet. "Hello?" Sylvie called out again as she stepped into the room with some concern. "Diana, is everything all right?"

Sylvie flipped the light switch. A couple of lamps came on, filling the room with the muted light that was customary in those hotels she'd known and that always made the room feel uncomfortably dim upon stepping into it from the more brightly lit hallway. It was still enough light to immediately see that Diana's "room" was a suite. On the one hand, that wasn't surprising for someone with Diana's star power. On the other hand, it was a bit surprising that their little convention had that luxury in the budget for her. Maybe someone connected to the hotel was a fan, too, and they'd swung the suite the same way Sylvie had arranged the use of the limo.

This wasn't a luxury penthouse or anything. It wasn't that kind of hotel. The room was spacious, though, and nicely furnished, even if most of the furniture had been pulled back to the walls to make room for a large, circular folding table in the middle of the room surrounded by five matching chairs, two of them overturned. A partially melted candle mounted on a cheesy skull-shaped holder rested on the table in front of each chair. Reflective tape on the table drew lines between the skulls, resulting in a five-pointed star design. A stack of well-worn fantasy paperbacks had been left on the kitchen counter beside a small pile of folders that matched the one on the floor. The papers looked like scripts, character sheets, and similar handouts for a role-playing game. Some pencils and a couple of small velvet bags for holding dice completed the impression that Diana had either hosted or was preparing to host a role-playing session with the sort of mystical atmosphere that would be appreciated by her fans. Was this what she'd invited Sylvie for? As a player to fill an empty slot in a game? Regardless, Sylvie *had* been invited, so she allowed the door to swing closed as she moved in for a closer look.

Nothing else looked out of place so, without thinking, she righted the overturned chairs and picked up the scattered papers, shoving them back into the folder and dropping it onto the pile on the counter. She traced the scent of incense to a castle-shaped incense holder on a side table. It was still smoking and still bore a price tag. It had probably come straight up from the dealer room. She traced the music to an old MP3 player and a compact set of speakers near the windowsill. She was debating between the urge to turn off the unattended music and the urge to not touch other peoples' stuff when a peal of cathedral bells from the next room made her jump. Had it been sound effects queued up for the game, or had it just come from a television? And had someone just turned it on, or was it on a timer? Sylvie composed herself and went to knock on the closed door to that room as the bells continued to ring. "Diana? It's Sylvie. You invited me up, remember?" Nothing.

Sylvie waited for a thirty-count. The bells kept ringing. She knocked again. Called out again. The bells trailed off into silence. She waited another thirty-count. Knocked again. Called again. She decided the sound had to have been on a timer, and she pushed the door open. No lights. She fumbled around for a light switch on the far side of the door but without success. From what she could see, the room appeared to be undergoing remodeling. They'd ripped out the carpets, the air smelled dusty, and the sound of her voice echoed a bit off the bare walls as she called out Diana's name again. Was this how they got a discount-rate suite for Diana? She'd have thought it just made the suite unsafe for renting out.

She pulled out her phone again and set it to flashlight mode, looking for the light switch. What she found was that no one was remodeling the room. It looked like an attic storeroom, raw and unfinished, supported with exposed wooden beams. Wooden crates and old trunks with rusting latches lined the walls. A thick layer of dust and cobwebs covered everything. Several sets of footprints crisscrossed the floor through the dust. Why would any hotel rent out a suite with an unlocked door into a disused storeroom that looked older than the hotel itself? Or was Diana just that eccentric that she'd paid the hotel to stage the most elaborate haunted-house live-action game set Sylvie had ever seen? The closed door on the far wall even looked like it had been pulled off of some very old house.

As Sylvie prepared to step into the room, she was suddenly struck with the skin-crawling feeling that this was the part of the movie where the innocent victim found the door slamming and locking behind her, trapping her in with the evil spirit so she could be slaughtered in the film's prologue and set the scene for the arrival of the real heroes. At the last moment, she quietly closed the door instead of entering, tucked away the key card, turned off her phone light, and slipped back out into the hall to search for Diana.

There was no sign of Diana in the lobby. Sylvie imagined several different possible conversations asking after her at the front desk. All of them ended with Sylvie surrendering the key card before she found out anything useful. She wasn't ready to let go of that option just yet. She moved on to check the lounge in the main hall but found it occupied by only a few tables full of late-night gamers.

"Hey, Lenore!" she greeted the one game master she recognized. "Sorry to interrupt. Has Diana Taylor been through here?"

The pink-haired young woman shook her head. The pink wasn't a costume. That was just Lenore. Pink hair, pink lipstick, pink eye shadow, pink athletic shoes, pink t-shirt adorned with the glittery words "Goth Princess" as a concession to the vampire-loving parents who remained inconsolable that their daughter had grown up hating the color black. Not that they considered her a total loss. After all, at this very moment she was hiding behind a home-made game master screen plastered with a collage of images from the *Dark Legacy* television series. They probably wished she identified less with the show's brother-sister monster-hunting duo and more with those creatures of the night that they fought, but at least she'd fallen in love with something thematically appropriate. "You missed Diana's nine-o'clock panel? I didn't see you there."

"I did," Sylvie sighed. "Too many places to be, too few of me to be in them. You know how it goes."

"Sorry about that." Lenore offered her a lopsided smile of sympathy. "It was great. Looked like they were recording it, though. You should definitely check it out."

"Any idea where she went after?" Sylvie asked.

"She's probably in her room," Lenore said. "I heard she's hosting one of her invitation-only games tonight. Maybe they could ring her for you at the desk?"

Sylvie briefly considered asking Lenore to come have a look at the odd room with her, but that wouldn't have endeared either of them to her table full of players, so Sylvie just thanked her and headed for the movie room. As Sylvie walked away, Lenore was throwing herself into the role of some sorceress her players needed to outwit, chanting a faux-Latin ritual she'd probably memorized from the show.

The current occupants of the movie room turned out to be a few people engaged in the tradition of heckling a really bad old film aided by some combination of mental fatigue and alcohol. None of them was Diana or anyone else she recognized, and Sylvie hesitated to step into the middle of their one-sided conversation with the screen. That just left the various room parties. Sylvie stopped back by the front desk to see where a bit of late-night noise had been sanctioned for the sake of filling up the hotel with convention goers, then she began wandering the halls, knocking on any doors with signs that invited it, asking after Diana. The first and second doors turned up nothing. The third turned up Brian instead.

"Well, that was quick," he said. "In my fantasies you two didn't come up for air until the morning. Or did you just chicken out?"

"Mind. Gutter. Not helpful," Sylvie sighed. "She never showed. She's not in her room. I'm running out of places to look and I'm a little worried. If she doesn't show up for her events tomorrow, NoNaCon's going to a take a big hit to its reputation and maybe a big hit financially. Plus, I found something...weird."

"Weird?" Brian cocked an eyebrow.

"Really weird. 'You'll never believe me, so I've just got to show you' weird," Sylvie said. "Can I lure you away from the party for a few?"

The event didn't seem to be anyone's idea of an epic party, so a short elevator ride later found them back at Diana's door. Sylvie knocked and called out a couple of times again before letting them in herself.

"Whoa!" Brian's jaw dropped. "I was mostly just trying to wind you up, but Diana Taylor straight up gave you her room key?"

"Not exactly." Sylvie brushed off the question. "I'll explain later. Can we stay focused on the weird bit?"

"A hot movie star inviting you up to her room isn't exactly mundane," he pointed out.

"Focus," Sylvie repeated, waving him to follow to the interior door as the outer door latched behind them. Sylvie reached for the door handle but froze as she realized that this was the part of the movie where the odd room vanished to be replaced by an ordinary hotel bedroom containing aforementioned hot actress in some sort of embarrassing moment. She aborted the move and knocked on the inner door instead, calling out again. She waited through another prolonged silence before finally opening the door again. The odd room hadn't vanished. Sylvie pulled out her phone and lit up the storeroom for Brian. "What do you make of it?"

"Yeah. Okay." Brian nodded, pulling out his own phone and tapping on the light. "That does seem kinda...out of place."

"Weirder," Sylvie said, "before I opened the door the first time, I heard bells from in here. Like cathedral bells. I thought it was a television or something, but...do you see any television?"

Brian shook his head as he pushed his way on into the room. His fingers brushed a line through the dust on top of one of the trunks, and he held them up for inspection. Sylvie was careful to keep him in sight as she backed up toward the circular table, found one of the chairs by touch, and dragged it over to wedge it into the doorway before joining him. She'd watched too many movies, read too many books, played too many games to take these sorts of things for granted. The moment you decided something out of place was harmless was the moment it suddenly took your head off. If the ongoing plot called for this door to close and lock with her on the other side, she was going to make the narrative work for it.

While Sylvie was indulging her paranoia, Brian tested a few of the trunks and found them locked. "What's through there?" he asked, nodding to the far door.

Sylvie shrugged. "I haven't looked."

"Really?" Brian cocked an eyebrow while he stared at her handiwork wedging the door open. "Isn't this stuff your catnip? I thought you were an adrenaline junkie."

"Sure," Sylvie agreed, finally heading for the door. "But a girl only gets to jump out of a plane without a parachute once. I'm looking forward to at least three or four leaps."

"I think you could survive jumping out of a storeroom without a parachute," Brian chuckled, still poking around to see if any of the containers might come open easily.

Sylvie tested the door, found it unlocked, and pushed it open a little warily. Before she could take in what lay beyond, something moved. *Someone* moved—quickly. Sylvie's body was already reacting before her mind could process the information.

The door had opened onto some sort of landing, dimly lit from below in addition to the stronger light of her phone. A man stood just beyond the door, his feet firmly planted as he swung one arm up toward her. Its hand held a pistol. "Don't—" the man began gruffly. Then Sylvie's hand caught his wrist, shoving the gun aside. Her other arm came up. The heel of her open palm drove hard into the man's nose, eliciting a loud crack. As the man crumpled to the floor, clutching his nose,

Sylvie's aghast brain caught up with the realization she'd just decked a fellow steampunk cosplayer wielding a toy revolver. Then her brain did another round of processing, took in the smell of gunpowder, took in Brian's yelp, and whipped her body around to find blood oozing through Brian's fingers where they'd clutched at his arm. Without breaking momentum, she let the spin carry her the rest of the way through a one-eighty-degree turn and she stomped on the man's wrist before yanking the revolver out of his hand. Melodrama demanded she turn the weapon back in its owner's face, but as far as Sylvie was concerned melodrama could go hang itself. Melodrama never wound up having to prove self-defense in a court of law when something accidentally went bang. Abstract concepts could be self-righteously annoying that way.

So, fighting off the impulse, Sylvie sent the gun skittering away across the floor as she sank over the man in a crouch, and she drew her wand instead. As a token concession to melodrama, she shoved it toward his face with a warning spark of electricity . Even as she did it, she suspected the move had no real intimidation value. The man's eyes remained closed as he fought back the combined shocks of a possibly broken nose and a brutalized wrist.

"You okay?" Sylvie asked Brian, sparing a glance back over her shoulder. "How bad is it?"

He was staring at her, slack-jawed. "I, uh...'ve been shot," he said, his brain clearly still running to catch up. "Not cool."

"How bad?" Sylvie repeated.

"Flesh wound?" he ventured uncertainly, lifting his hand enough to peer beneath. "I think."

Sylvie felt the man start to twist beneath her and she set off another warning spark in his face. This time she was sure he saw it. He went still.

"The hotel's got a security guard," Sylvie snapped at Brian. "Get him. Have the front desk send him up here and get someone to look at that arm. I've got this."

"I...Yeah. Okay," Brian said, still seeming disoriented but enough with it to add, "Remind me to stay on your good side."

"Stay on my good side," she told him. "Now go." He went. She silently reassured herself he would be fine. All he had to do was make it to the hall. After that, even if he fainted, the night was still young enough that there would be convention-goers along every few minutes. He'd get any help he needed and would probably send her help too.

"Talk fast," Sylvie said, turning her attention back to the man. "Where's Diana?" This time she consciously indulged the call of the melodrama. Whenever she tried to role-play an intimidating character, she did it by conjuring up one part anger and one part theater. Right now there was no need to conjure the anger; it was already there and fighting to be unleashed. Awareness of just how closely those last few seconds had skirted total disaster fueled a fear in her that further fueled the anger in its turn. She had speed and grace, yes. She couldn't count the number of times she'd been fruitlessly entreated to pursue dance as a calling. She also packed more strength than most people expected from a woman of her size. All that and her self-defense training together, though, would have counted for nothing if the man hadn't been sloppy and stupid. He never should have tried to intimidate her with a gun literally in her face instead of pointing it at her from three or four yards away.

"Who?" the man groaned.

"Diana Taylor," Sylvie enunciated carefully. "Lark Starling?" The man was older than the core audience that had grown up on the *Lovelace* books and movies. Threads of silver laced his short, dark beard. Still, no fantasy fan attending a convention in full costume could be completely oblivious to the *Lovelace* phenomenon. His continued blank look betrayed him as some sort of ringer in fan camouflage. Had she walked into the middle of a celebrity kidnapping scheme? If so, she couldn't assume this man was operating alone. Did he have friends who'd heard the gunshot?

She abruptly pushed up and away from the man to get clear of his reach, stowing the wand on her belt even as she reached for the pepper spray with her other hand. "Stay down," she demanded as she edged toward the stairs that headed down from the landing and—with a quick flash of her phone light—satisfied herself that she wasn't about to get overrun from below. In the process she also confirmed that the architecture here made even less sense than the architecture in the storeroom. This wasn't the landing at the top of a neat little emergency stair tucked into the space between hotel rooms. This was a wooden landing at the top of a wooden stair with an old-fashioned wooden railing between it and the open air of some dark-but-spacious room. Try as she might, she couldn't make the place fit into her mental map of the hotel.

"There was four other wibbin here a bid ago," the nasally impaired man managed. "I chucked theb all oud the frond door ondo the sdreed. Didn'd ask their nabes."

"*You're* the security guard?" Sylvie asked, appalled. "Costuming? Maybe next time staying in uniform would save you a bloody nose." She suddenly found herself regretting the reflexive assault again, hoping the nose was only bloodied and not broken. She started to ask what he was doing in Diana's room—then stopped herself, realizing he'd been standing outside the room. More questions began to queue up in a disorderly fashion, fighting for priority until she settled on, "Where's your I.D. badge?"

"By whad?" he asked.

"I just want some proof you're supposed to be lurking around here with a gun before I relax, okay?"

"Whad are *you* doig here?" he asked a bit indignantly, though it was clear in his face he was no longer feeling in charge of the situation.

"I am a guest," she replied tartly, pulling out the key card and waving it at him. "Of the convention," she amended, belatedly remembering it wasn't her key card at all.

"The conbenchun?" He didn't sound reassured. If anything he was sounding more nervous. "I'b jusd doig a job, okay? I dond ged paid buch, I dond ask quesdiods, and nobody tells be buch. I cad show you where the wibbin wend—then you're gone, I'b doig by job and nobody else geds hurd. Okay?"

"Yeah. Okay," Sylvie decided after a moment's thought, reassuring herself that seeing the convention guest of honor was unharmed and ready to show in the morning had to be top priority. Hopefully the rest of what was going on would explain itself. She pulled out a handkerchief from the emergency costuming kit she'd incorporated into a belt pouch of the steampunk outfit and tossed it to him.

"Thaks," he said sincerely, trying to staunch the steady trickle of blood from his nose. "Cub on." He climbed cautiously to his feet and headed down the stairs. The flight led down to a balcony that ran along the perimeter of the large room, the whole space lit by nothing more than a few widely spaced candles flickering in sconces along the walls.

Candles, Sylvie reflected. *The haunted house theme continues.* It wasn't just in the candles, either. It was there in the dusty carpets and the ornate banisters and the period portraits lining the walls. If she'd been given an unlimited budget and told, "Go build a really old-looking haunted house set for a live-action game," it would have come out looking something like this. The cost would be incredible, though. More than that, Sylvie knew this hotel pretty well. It weighed in at a grand total of five floors and possessed a footprint that she could circle in ten minutes without even hurrying. There was no major construction going on and no remodeling visible from the outside.

She'd even seen the floor plan and toured every room of available convention space while helping out during the planning phase for this year's NoNaCon. The balcony she was standing on and the room she was standing in did not exist. All of which meant…what? Any normal human would simply rationalize it away but Sylvie found herself full of glorious conclusions she could hardly resist jumping to.

"I'm Sylvie," she finally said as she followed the man along the balcony toward another, larger stair that led on down toward the main floor of the room. "Can I ask your name?"

"Id's Dewey, ba'ab." He gave a ginger little nod as he glanced back at her.

"Did any of these women have dark skin, dark eyes, black hair?" Sylvie asked.

"A cubble, yeah." Dewey agreed.

"Rather pretty?" Sylvie asked.

"Oh, yeah," Dewey said without hesitation. "All of theb. You'd have fid ride in." He gave Sylvie a little grin and she felt the heat rising in her cheeks despite herself. "Freds of yours?"

"Hopefully," Sylvie said. "At least one."

They stepped onto the main floor, and Dewey led the way past dust-cloth-covered lumps of furniture to what promised to be an outer door. On the way there Sylvie decided the place was, in fact, one coat-of-arms and a couple of suits of armor shy of being the perfect haunted house; but otherwise it still seemed to pass muster. Dewey opened the big door and gestured broadly for her to exit. Beyond the door, a short flight of stone steps led down to a walkway across a token expanse of grass to a wrought-iron gate in a wrought-iron fence. Past the fence lay no sign of the hotel parking lot—just a narrow cobblestone street shrouded in fog and lit by flickering, old-fashioned gas lamps.

"Look, Dewey," Sylvie said, pausing at the doorway. "How many doors are there into that storeroom?"

"Just the...one." He paused uncertainly.

"Then where did my friend go?" she asked. "The one who got shot? Did you see him leave?"

"There's no door there," Dewey insisted.

"But you saw it anyway?"

"I...Yeah," he finally admitted, to himself as much as to Sylvie.

"I don't understand it either. It shouldn't be there. I shouldn't have been able to come through it. Its being there may cause you more trouble. Do you have anything I can write a note on?" Sylvie had no doubt she could have found a note pad back in Diana's room, but returning to get it would have been the part of the movie where—propped open or not—the door would have flickered and disappeared on her, leaving her stranded back where everything made mundane sense. She couldn't risk that. Not yet. She had to find Diana. Even more than that, she had to understand what sort of adventure she'd finally stumbled into after the adult world had nearly beaten all belief in magic out of her.

"So are these gizbos your own inbentions?" Dewey asked as they searched around for a writing desk. "That's a ride powerful lide." He nodded toward her phone and the illumination it provided.

"We really should find someone to take a look at your nose," Sylvie said with a sigh, partly to divert the new direction of the conversation. She wasn't convinced yet that explaining the technology she was lugging along would be a good plan. "Is there a...medic somewhere nearby I could send over to see you when I leave?"

Dewey shook his head gingerly. "I've took worse in bar fides. Id was already crooked. Jusd led me say you was sub bruiser three tibes your waid and half again as dall 'sdead of a slip of a wubbin whud snuck in in her unmendshunables." He grinned.

Sylvie blushed. Between the rush of events and the serendipity that this man's outfit could pass for steampunk, she'd been rolling with the assumption that she'd blend wherever this was. That didn't take into account the fact that men's steampunk fashions just looked like embellished Victorian wear while women's steampunk fashions tended to look a lot more like what a fashionable lady of the 1890s might have worn under her dress. If the world outside that front door followed at all closely to the historical nineteenth century and she wasn't safely off the streets before sun-up, there was no doubt her outfit would cause an instant scandal. Now *that* would be some serious adrenaline.

Picturing it, she couldn't suppress a giggle. The reaction only broadened Dewey's grin. Sylvie thought briefly about confiding in him that women showing off their legs like this was pretty normal on her side of the store-room door, but that might just be begging him to go see for himself. She wasn't sure that would be a good idea. Maybe if the door still worked after she found Diana she'd invite him to go have a look to make up for what she'd done to his nose. Until then... "That's not a complaint, is it?" she asked instead. "About the unmentionables, I mean."

Dewey barked out a short laugh. "No," he said decisively. "No."

"Good." Sylvie grinned. "'Cause I'm rather proud of my legs. I'd hate to find they don't measure up after all."

"If you're one of theb dance hall girls, just poid be do the frund row."

"You're sweet, but no. I'm just a girl who likes an appreciative eye on her. Ah, here's what we need." She coughed at the cloud of dust that billowed up as she pulled the cover back from the writing desk. It was still stocked with paper.

Sylvie didn't even check for a pen or the ink supply. She always kept a ballpoint mixed in with the gear on this costume, and she wouldn't know how to use an older style pen if she found one. She made a point of leaning over the desk at an angle that would give her new friend a good view while she wrote—but that would also keep him in her peripheral vision. They weren't *that* friendly, after all. Besides, she wanted the satisfaction of watching him watch her. She took her time over the note, then finally presented it to Dewey.

"Tack it to the other side of the door that doesn't exist or some such," she said wryly. "I wouldn't step through, though. The trouble with things that can't exist is you never know how they'll behave. Hopefully this will stop anyone else from coming through and complicating your night. Now, I believe I promised to leave?"

Dewey escorted Sylvie back to the front door and pointed off down the street. "They was headed thad way," he said. "Toward Bellraben Cathedral. Good place to sdard lookig. Sure you're gonna be all ride oud dressed like thad?"

A part of her wasn't. She'd had it drilled into her head all her life not to go walking alone down a dark, unfamiliar street no matter how she was dressed. Still, she was loaded for bear, easily underestimated, and heading off through a parkour playground. The chances of running into anyone she couldn't get away from struck her as slim to none under the circumstances.

"I'll be fine." She smiled. She kept smiling until he closed the door—then she turned to face the foggy street and drew in a heavy, bracing breath. The only direct evidence now that she wasn't the only person in the world was a few voices too distant to make out any words from. Under the circumstances, that was a little bit comforting and a lot scary. Whatever else was true, though, the laws of physics as she knew them had been violated to drop her someplace she had no right to be. Nothing could drag her away from that.

She turned off her phone light, palmed her pepper spray in one hand, took her police baton in the other, and strode silently off down the cobblestone street.

CHAPTER THREE
Our Story So Far

Oddly enough, Sylvie had never actually seen nineteenth-century London, but the street and the residences along it did a good job of approximating the mental image of it she had pieced together through popular culture. This seemed to be a wealthier neighborhood, where it was mostly garden walls and not the buildings themselves that pressed in against the street. Ahead through the fog she could just make out a towering silhouette that had to be the cathedral in question. Surely it also housed the pealing bells she'd heard earlier.

As the street jogged and turned and split off in random directions, Sylvie kept the cathedral in her sight. She also left a lipstick arrow at each intersection to mark the way she'd come, grateful once again that she was wearing the costume with all the well-stocked pockets. It made her feel like a steampunk superhero prowling the night with her utility belt. A couple of times voices and footfalls warned her in plenty of time to duck into the shadows and wait quietly for passersby to keep on passing. A few of the residences had lights flickering in a window or two. Mostly the signs of life remained distant and muted, though it did sound like she was drawing closer to an area with a bit more night life. Then a whir and a clank from up ahead startled Sylvie and she ducked back into the shadows.

More whirring and clanking followed. The sounds grew gradually closer until a spindly, wheeled arrangement of mechanical limbs came bumping over the cobblestones, sweeping the street with oversized brooms and spearing trash on short, sharp spikes. From her hiding place in the alley, Sylvie couldn't see any sign of an operator—or even any place on the contraption to put one. A robot then. She really had fallen into a steampunk city. She watched the thing trundle on, shoving debris into sewer drains and depositing trash into a basket attached to the central body. Whatever sensors it was equipped with she couldn't identify, but if it knew she was there at all it paid her no mind. Still, she remained in the alley until the thing became a whirring, clanking silhouette about to vanish in the fog.

"Yeah," a voice at her feet said. "They give me the willies, too. Are you Sylvie, then?"

Sylvie looked warily down to find a small, leopard-spotted cat gazing back up at her. It wore a collar studded with stones that shimmered when the lamp light caught them. "Ummm...I *am* Sylvie," she said.

"Lovely," the cat replied. "I was told you might be showing up."

"Yes!" Sylvie hissed, casting her eyes skyward with an enthusiastic fist-pump. "A talking cat!"

"Amazing how few people share your instant enthusiasm," the cat said with a twitch of its ears. "They usually just go through this whole disbelief routine—try to blame it on drink or some such. Thanks for skipping over that bit."

"You're more than welcome," Sylvie said amiably. "I've been waiting pretty much my whole life for impossible things to start happening. I'm not about to risk explaining them away now that they have. The thought I might succeed is just too awful to bear. So who are you exactly?"

"An associate of Diana Taylor's," the cat said. "I accept the name Loki. No relation beyond the basic symbolism."

"So you're a bringer of chaos?" Sylvie asked.

"I see no point in allowing life to stagnate. Anyway, the Diana's in need of a discrete, thumb-enabled personage and was hoping you'd turn out to be observant and curious enough to wind up here."

"She did promise me an adventure," Sylvie replied.

"Ah, well. I don't expect this is the adventure she'd meant," the cat said. "Her evening went rather abruptly sidewise and now she's on one side of a locked door and the key is on the other. This place wasn't on her agenda at all."

"All this begs so many questions I don't know where to start," Sylvie said.

"Perhaps you should start with walking," Loki suggested. "I expect the Diana would appreciate some haste."

"Sure." Sylvie nodded. "Lead the way."

Loki turned and trotted off down the street, back the way she'd come. "You overshot," he explained. "I've been following you a while to decide if you might just be a local."

"Are you a local?" Sylvie asked, falling in behind the cat.

"Me? No. All the local cats seem to be as lingually challenged as your world's are," Loki said.

"So where do you come from then?" she asked.

"My world, naturally." Loki turned down an alley and led the way to a small garden gate in a tall brick wall. He slipped easily through the wrought-iron grillwork, but when Sylvie went to follow him she found it locked. "Now that's odd," the cat remarked. "Did he lock that too?"

"He?" Sylvie asked.

"A man. Human. 'Marvin' or some such. All rats in the attic, but I guess he'd charmed one of the ladies into bringing him into the Diana's room with her. The Diana knew him, wasn't too pleased to see him even before he started demanding she open the door here. Pulled a gun when she tried to throw him out."

Sylvie scrambled easily up a drainpipe on the building across the alley, kicked off the brickwork, and broke her momentum by touching down briefly on top of the garden wall before dropping lightly down inside.

"I'm impressed," Loki said as she landed. "That was practically feline of you."

Sylvie allowed herself a little grin of satisfaction as she dropped a theatrical curtsy at the compliment. "I think I've got a real shot at getting onto one of those extreme-obstacle-course TV shows. Going to try anyway. So 'Marvin'? Not 'Martin' was it? Please tell me it wasn't Martin Kight." But she already had a sinking feeling she hadn't been mistaken about glimpsing the actor earlier. She'd had a thing for Diana's bad-boy *Lovelace* co-star back in the day, but his off-screen image had become tarnished too since the last of the films had wrapped. She wasn't sure now what to make of him. There'd been no accusations of pulling guns, but the behavior wasn't otherwise out of line with who the tabloids made him out to be these days.

The cat flipped its ears noncommittally. "I couldn't say." Then he cocked his head, listening as he peered into the darkness of the garden. "Human coming. Male. Adult. Probably local. Don't expect he's dangerous but might make a scene if he sees you here. Choose fast."

"Wait!" Sylvie hissed. "I still don't know..." But Loki had already disappeared into the greenery. She still didn't know *anything* really, and certainly not enough to make any sort of decent plan out of. She could get back out of the garden easily enough, but she didn't know how much time she had. The wall was tall enough that the quickest reliable way she could spot involved scaling the gate directly, and that would make a good bit of noise. If the man was at all close he'd at least know someone had left in a hurry—and that would make returning problematic for her. There were places to hide, but she couldn't see at all well, and she didn't know which direction he'd be coming from. Discovery would be a real concern and, again, that could lead to a dicey situation. No, she couldn't let the cat panic her into thinking like a cat. She wasn't a cat. She was a woman bracing herself to deal with a man. That was something she knew how to do.

One thing easily visible in the night was a stone bench set close to the garden path. She settled herself on it and fished the digest-sized NoNaCon convention booklet out of her largest belt pouch. Crossing her legs artfully and flicking on her phone light to read by, she opened the schedule to a random page and began studying an advertisement for a vintage comic bookstore with grave intensity, until she heard someone clear his throat. "Oh. Hello," she said in her most disarming tone as she looked up. "Are you a friend of Miss Taylor's?"

"I, uh...I'm sorry," the man said, eying Sylvie's outfit. "Is this *that* kind of party?"

"It *could* be." She grinned at him. She wasn't half kidding. The man could have been a walking advertisement for a period romance novel, all roguish swashbuckling good looks in a domino mask and a costume that looked more "King's Musketeers" than Victorian gentleman. "I can't show my face in a masquerade without a costume, so I've decided to improvise. Do you like it?" She stood up and twirled for him, partly to keep him off-balance, partly for the fun of it.

The man laughed. "What I can see of it in this light, yes. Is...everything all right out here? I thought I heard, well...shouting." She wasn't sure she had him off-balance. If anything, he seemed to be relaxing. She clearly had his attention, though, and he didn't seem eager to call her out or anything, so it was all good. Besides, the gentlemen here had now gone two-for-two on letting a girl be dressed down and a bit flirty without jumping straight into getting crude and demanding. That in itself was almost as good as a talking cat.

"I haven't heard anything," Sylvie said. "I've just been enjoying the quiet. Haven't been here long, though." She turned off her phone and tucked it away, hoping to keep the man from getting any more curious about it than Dewey had been.

"All right, then," the man said with a shrug. "Sorry to bother you." He started to go but paused and turned back with a grin. "Although what was it you were saying about this turning into *that* sort of party?"

"Just that I like dressing like this." Her eyes sparkled with mischief. "Sometimes even less. So much easier to move. So nice letting my skin breathe. I'm game for that sort of party if the other ladies are."

"Even less, you say?" The man's mask might as well have been transparent for all the good it did hiding his intrigued expression.

"Even...less," Sylvie breathed huskily. She was *liking* this game. Then the sight of Loki sitting behind the man, twitching his tail impatiently, brought her back to the job at hand, and she forced herself to shift gears. "Oh, is that your cat?" she asked suddenly, breaking the moment. "I love cats."

"What?" the man asked. She could practically hear the screeching of his mental brakes as he turned to look down. "No. Not mine."

"Maybe that's what you heard," Sylvie said. "Wait. Does it want us to follow it?"

Loki, who hadn't moved, just glared at her for several seconds before letting out an audible sigh then getting up and trotting off down the garden path.

"I think It does. Come on." She grabbed the man's hand and pulled him along with her. He offered no protest. If having a local along made this rescue awkward, so be it. She was having too much fun to just walk away. Anyway, wasn't a girl marching off on a quest in a magical new world supposed to acquire three companions? She was sure there was a rule about that. Hopefully she could fill out her quota with a robot or something. "Oh," she added as they hurried along. "I'm Sylvie. You?"

"Ummm...mask?" The man gestured to his half-concealed face.

"Do you think this cat is leading us back to the masquerade?" Sylvie asked pointedly.

"I guess not," he admitted.

"Do you think I'm going to wind up wearing any less than this if you won't even tell me your name?"

"Fair point," he said. "I'm Alban." She rewarded him with a bright smile.

They arrived at an old garden shed, where Loki paused for a moment before trotting around the side and hopping up to slip in through a broken window.

"Do cats really ask people to follow them?" Alban asked.

"I don't know about 'people'," Sylvie said, "but they ask me." She went back to try the shed door. It opened easily, but the interior was close enough to pitch black that it might as well have been. She pulled out her phone again and turned on the light.

"That's quite the gadget," Alban said. "Nice, strong, steady beam. And I've never seen controls like that. Did you make it?"

"Not helpful," she admonished him as she peered into the shed. "Cat first, then flirting. If there's time after we can talk gadgets."

"Are you sure about the cat?" he asked.

"Pretty sure," Sylvie said. "I think it must be Diana's—Miss Taylor's." She cast the light about the old shed, falling on nothing but dirt and cobwebs and the expected gardening implements until she angled it toward the floor. A trap door in the far corner lay open. A ladder led down into darkness. Loki, who had been waiting on the trap door, hopped onto the wooden rungs and began the awkward business of a controlled descent with claws that, like any cat's, really curved the wrong way for the job.

"And are you sure you want to go down there?" Alban asked.

"No. But I'm doing it," Sylvie said. "It's narratively safe."

"It's *what*?" He cocked an eyebrow.

"Narratively safe. Sure, someone might come along and lock me in, but the tension's all wrong for me to not find a way out if that happens. And if there's no narrator it'd be pretty far-fetched to have someone lurking in the shadows just waiting for me to stumble along so they could lock me in here, right? Either way my odds are good for now."

"Did that make any sense at all?" Alban asked.

"Don't tell me you've seriously never felt like there was someone or something just out of sight pulling strings in your life for the sake of entertainment? Theirs, I mean, not yours?"

"Events do seem inclined to...conspire, if that's what you mean," Alban admitted. "Like the world never seems content to have just one thing go wrong at a time. It much prefers threes at the least."

"There you go," Sylvie said. "Some people read holy books for clues on how to deal with that feeling. I look to narrative tropes. It's worked okay so far." She promptly scooted down to the lip of the opening and lowered herself onto the ladder, shining her flashlight downward. In all, it looked like about a fifteen-foot descent to a flagstone floor. She descended in three short drops, catching herself one-handed the first two times so that she never had to stash her phone light. "Keep a watch from up there if you like," she called back. "Could come in handy." He was already sliding down onto the ladder, though, and soon joined her at the bottom.

"I've never been one to let an adventure walk away," Alban said, surveying the small room with Sylvie as she shone the light around. The same size and shape as the room above, it just seemed to be a brick-walled cellar for the shed, only odd in that Sylvie couldn't recall ever seeing a shed with a cellar before and in having a tunnel out in one wall. The tunnel was narrow enough she'd barely be able to use it without turning sideways. Loki sat waiting for her about twenty feet down the tunnel. When he seemed satisfied she'd noticed, he turned and continued on. She desperately wanted to question the cat, but he seemed unwilling to speak up in front of a local, and she couldn't convince herself that was a bad call.

Before long, the tunnel opened out into a circular chamber with other tunnels opening off of it like an old railway round house. Loki headed off down one that was noticeably broader than the others. Sylvie pulled out her lipstick again and marked the tunnel they'd come out of before following the cat.

"Do you do this a lot?" Alban asked.

"Since I was twelve," Sylvie answered automatically. That was when she'd sat down with her friends over summer break and began exploring her first monster-filled labyrinth armed only with a character sheet and a fist full of dice. Scores of adventures later, the games had taught her an amazing number of things, some of them actually useful. "How about you?"

"I've explored my share of tunnels, I guess," Alban said, "but I don't feel as confident about it as you act."

"A maze is a maze is a maze. The important bit is not taking your own memory or power of perception for gran...ted." Sylvie's voice trailed to a stuttering halt as they stepped out onto a balcony overlooking a broad, open-roofed circular space like a grand arena. "Is that a roller coaster?"

"Yeah," Alban answered. "Have you never been to Poppikin Park?"

"Is that what this is?" Sylvie asked. Most of what she could see was shadows and silhouettes. Starlight reduced the rest to only subtle shades of gray. Even so, those silhouettes and shades of gray screamed "amusement park"—not a gaudy modern theme park, but an old-fashioned, wholesome-looking affair that evoked visions of parasol-toting ladies strolling arm-in-arm with gentlemen wearing straw hats and armed with bamboo canes, while amazingly well-mannered but thoroughly excited children dashed from attraction to attraction. The silhouette of a Ferris wheel was unmistakable. Another silhouette was likely that of a carousel. The roller coaster didn't swoop or soar beyond anything that might show up at a modest state fair, but it did seem to completely circle the park. *And it was a roller coaster on another world!*

"I practically grew up here," Alban said, though Sylvie was too busy shining her phone light around in a vain attempt to brighten up the park to catch his accompanying expression or body language. "Born and raised not ten minutes away by foot. I'd no idea about this tunnel though."

"Is it still open?" Sylvie demanded. "During the day I mean. Will they turn everything on in the morning?"

Alban leaned back against the railing and turned his head to study her. "And if I said yes?"

"I've got to see it," she said without hesitation. "I've got to ride everything."

"They might expect you to...wear a bit more." Alban chuckled.

"Their loss." Sylvie smirked.

"And mine," Alban sighed. "Would you be willing to wait a little longer if it meant you could stay dressed down?"

Sylvie laughed and met his gaze with a naughty grin. "Maybe. Did you have something in mind?"

"Maybe." Alban met her grin with a more restrained smile, but his eyes still sparkled. "The city is full of secrets. I know my fair share if not more—but sharing secrets requires some trust, does it not? And here we've barely met."

"Do *not* think you can go dangling the promise of mischievous secrets and then simply yank it away," Sylvie admonished him. "I've killed men for less."

"Seriously?" Alban asked, taken aback.

"Not at all," Sylvie sighed. "But I would've if looks could kill, so close enough to base a wild story on. Anyway, spill or I'll pull on real clothes at the first opportunity. You might never see my legs again."

"I stand nigh mortally wounded at the thought," Alban said, clutching a hand dramatically to his chest. "You win some concession at least. Have you ever heard of the Ministry of Misbehavior?"

"*Now* who's making stuff up?" Sylvie laughed.

"Again you wound me!" Alban gasped. "Its existence is a genuine bona fide rumor spread about by the finest gossips."

"Of which you are apparently one," Sylvie said with a grin.

"It would seem," Alban conceded. "But the thrust of the stories is this: there are some things people are going to do no matter how strictly they might be forbidden. Maybe it's indulging in opium or alcohol, maybe it's gambling, maybe it's something carnal—like a woman showing her legs." At that, Sylvie giggled. "When a crime has victims, okay. Doesn't matter if people will persist at it or not, you've still got to try to crack down on it. But do you know what comes of rabidly forbidding people to indulge in vices that harm no one but themselves?"

"I'll bet you're gonna tell me, aren't you?" Sylvie said, intentionally invading the periphery of his personal space as she turned to fully face him.

"It creates a hunting ground for the serious predators," Alban said. "An opium addict who knows he'll be cast out of polite society for admitting to his problem will be utterly at the mercy of anyone he gets his fix from—utterly at the mercy of anyone who knows he's even getting his fix at all if they aren't equally compromised to him. When addiction is considered a mortal sin instead of an illness, it creates this whole underworld ecosystem where the sharks of society feed off of the addicts without fear of justice. Whatever price the dealer chooses to exact that's the price the addict will pay. There's simply no end to it, and the hunting's so good that there will always be another shark rushing to claim the territory if it's vacated or if he simply thinks he can take it by force. Violence becomes inevitable, whole neighborhoods become unlivable, all for our refusal to forgive the original victimless crime."

"Yeah," Sylvie nodded. "The lessons of Prohibition." Seeing his slightly puzzled expression, she waved off her own comment. "So the Ministry of Misbehavior...?" she prompted to get the conversation moving again.

"The stories say it exists to create a sort of policed underworld where the perpetrators of victimless crime can turn for help or sometimes simply indulge without guilt."

"Oooh. So my own personal bodyguard, who would see I could ride a roller-coaster with bare legs? Like that?" Sylvie grinned flirtatiously. "Tell me more."

Alban leaned in closer, pressing well past the fringes of Sylvie's personal space. "If you could...would you?" he murmured, eyes locked with hers.

Sylvie could feel herself flushing at the intimacy. "Would you be there to see it if I did?" she murmured back, not shying from his gaze.

"Let's go with yes," Alban said, hovering close enough now for her to feel the warmth of his breath. "Would you do it?"

Sylvie swallowed. "Uh huh," she said, nodding slowly. "I'd like that." Never mind that she'd already done it dozens of times, wearing short skirts or short shorts when she'd climbed aboard taller, faster, far wilder-looking roller coasters than this. She'd never before had a charming stranger get in her face and make it sound shamelessly erotic. She might nearly as well have jabbed herself with her own wand for all the electricity that coursed through her body as his lips gently brushed hers. Sylvie was vaguely aware she'd let out a little moan.

"And don't think I've forgotten your mention about wearing less. If—"

"If we pretend I said I'd ride it nude, would you shut up and kiss me properly?" Sylvie interrupted in a sensual growl.

Loki chose that moment to let out an indignant, impatient yowl from his perch on the railing just beyond their arm's reach. Sylvie repaid it by fixing him with one of those if-looks-could-kill glares—then by grabbing Alban by the collar and pulling him into a kiss herself. She held it long and deep, fully indulging the wanton lure of it out of spite while she ran her hands through his hair and he ran his hands down her back on their way to places even lower. A detached part of Sylvie's brain marveled at her own behavior but also knew she was—essentially—roaring drunk, intoxicated on an adventure she'd been waiting to start for as long as she could remember.

When necessity finally forced her up for air, she pushed Alban away and turned her attention back to the cat. He'd adopted an air of long-suffering patience while he waited. "Right. Diana," Sylvie said. "Lead on."

"Let's be clear," Alban said as they hurried along the balcony and then down a winding metal stair with Sylvie's phone lighting the way. "Did you just say you'd get naked?"

"Not as such, no," Sylvia said. "Nor did you promise someone would run cover for me if I misbehave. So far it's all just flights of fancy. Good kiss though. We can build on that."

"Oh. Right. We'd been talking about the Ministry of Misbehavior," Alban said.

"Wait. Do you hear that?" Sylvie asked as they arrived at ground level behind the cover of a weeping willow on the banks of a pond. They listened through a few moments of silence before the thudding sound repeated. "Maybe we're getting close."

"To your friend?" Alban asked. "I'm still not terribly clear on why you even think she'd be in here. Or why we're following a cat."

"Well, *you're* following a cat hoping you'll get another chance to kiss me and maybe see more than my legs. Does the rest matter?" Sylvie asked cheerily.

"Not when you put it that way." Alban laughed. "How are my odds looking?"

"Pretty good," Sylvie said. "Especially on the kissing front. Are you going on the roller coaster with me?"

"Wouldn't miss it," Alban said.

"Even if I'm fully dressed?"

"Even if you're fully dressed."

"Good," Sylvie said. "Right answers."

"Not to brag," Alban said, "but I'm known far and wide for not being miserably incompetent at answering easy questions. It's a gift. Besides, the roller coaster is the best part of the park."

They walked past some booths of carnival-style games and a gaudy building that was surely some sort of funhouse. In the pale, monochrome light of the fog-shrouded night, the funhouse suffered the same disturbing effect as clown makeup caught in a black-and-white photo. What was surely a cheerful-looking building by the light of day simply struck Sylvie as haunted and creepy by night. She was more than slightly relieved when Loki led them on past it instead of into it.

Sylvie jumped once when a cleaning robot similar to the one she'd met on the street lurched suddenly to life only a few paces away, but then it wandered off down an intersecting path, sweeping as it went and seeming to pay them no mind. Finally they arrived at a facade meant to look like the front porch of a nice house, though it was hard to miss that the windows were fake and the door—if it wasn't fake too—would lead back into the wall of the grand pit that contained the park.

The thump came again, rattling the door of the facade. Loki sat waiting for them beside the door.

"Looks like we've arrived," Sylvie said as she mounted the steps up to the porch. "Diana? Is that you?" she called as she rapped gently on the door.

"Sylvie! It's Sylvie!"

The voice wasn't Diana's, but Sylvie recognized it in an instant. "Nami? What are you doing here?"

A chorus of female voices talking over each other poured out from behind the door until Diana's shushed the others into silence. "Lovely you could join us, Sylvie," she said. "But can we save all the catching up until after the door's open? Loki, are you there too?"

The cat hesitated for a moment, glancing between Alban and the door. Then he sighed resignedly and called back, "Yeah. I'll point her to the key." Alban did a double-take, staring down at the cat. "What?" Loki demanded. "It's not like anyone claimed I *couldn't* talk." He turned and trotted along the porch. "The key's here." He tapped a paw on a potted fern. "He hid it in the dirt."

"Did you know it could talk?" Alban asked Sylvie.

"Only after he introduced himself," Sylvie said. "Do you really need the mask still?" She tapped her cheek meaningfully. "We're not going back to the party, are we?"

"It would seem not," Alban agreed. "Might as well have one less thing to explain to your friends." He took off the mask and tucked it away inside his coat while Sylvie dug in the dirt. Without the mask he looked less roguish but no less handsome. She could live with that.

Key in hand, they returned to unlock the door. The room beyond seemed to be some sort of spartan utility space, but Sylvie didn't get much of a look at it before four women came spilling out. None of them stopped moving before they reached the green of the lawn. Then Manami spun about and gave Sylvie a tremendous hug. Diana didn't wait for them to finish it before joining in the hug. Then she seemed to realize for the first time that Alban was there. "And this would be...?"

"Alban Langridge." He introduced himself with a bow. "Concerned citizen. Are you all quite all right?"

"From the way you're staring," Diana said, "I'm going to guess you're a local rather than a cosplayer."

"Uhhh...yes," Alban replied slowly. "I am a local. I'm not even sure where Cozplay is." He had indeed been staring. Except for Diana, all the women—Manami, Felicity Ward, and a Latina Sylvie didn't recognize—were costumed in steampunk outfits at best only slightly less revealing than Sylvie's. Even Diana, who was still wearing the same casual, blue knee-length dress that she'd been wearing on the convention floor, didn't begin to blend with the Victorianish surroundings.

Diana sighed. "Are we freaking you out?" she asked Alban. "Please tell me if we're freaking you out."

"It's...No. I'm fine," Alban said. "Puzzled but fine. I guess you were at the costume party too?"

"Yes. Go with that explanation," Diana said with an emphatic gesture.

"Me too," Loki volunteered. "Lovely party."

Diana sighed again, rubbing her forehead. "I believe what you meant to say, Loki, was, 'Meow. Meow.'"

"Oh. Yes. Absolutely," Loki agreed. "That's what I meant. Not like you're the one who asked me to talk in front of him."

"Are we going to have any trouble over this, Mister Langridge?" Diana asked pointedly.

"Over...a talking cat?" he asked.

"Do you know—or have you heard of—any other talking cats?" Diana asked.

"Only if you count fairy stories," Alban said.

"My experience is that people can't be counted on to deal constructively with novelty," Diana said. "Most of them want the world to run smoothly down the same familiar track they've always traveled, free from jolts and surprises. The unaccountable gets ignored, shunned, exploited, or even sadistically persecuted. I'm very particular about who I introduce novelty to, Mister Langridge. If you find my friend disturbing—if you find *any* of us disturbing—I ask that you be on your way. We were brought here against our will and against my better judgment, so we'll conclude our business as rapidly as ever we may and disappear forever."

"What? All of you?" He glanced toward Sylvie with what she found to be a gratifying hint of dismay.

Sylvie couldn't offer much more than a shrug in response. "I hardly have a clue what's going on," she said.

"Well don't run off on my account," Alban said, raising open hands in a placating gesture. "I like novelty. I like cats. I like meeting spirited and slightly odd women. If they're as pretty as you and immodestly dressed, all the better. I'm a bit disoriented, yes, but I'm good. I'd much rather hear your story than run you off."

Diana studied him for a few moments through slightly narrowed eyes, then finally nodded. "Good enough," she said. Her demeanor softened somewhat, though her voice remained stern and formal. "We're all," she said, using her finger to hint at a circle in the air that seemed to include every woman plus the cat, "from another world. We came here by magic ritual, coerced by a former colleague. He stole something of mine and locked us in that storeroom. I intend to hunt him down, retrieve my property, then return us home. If you think I'm lying or crazy, again, please go. In any event, let that explanation suffice for now. I have work to do and the sands are running through the proverbial hourglass."

"I knew it!" Sylvie crowed. "You really *are* an enchantress!"

"I really *are* an enchantress," Diana admitted with a lopsided smile. "Sort of. Don't ask me for any of those *Lovelace* spells. For now, don't expect any spells at all."

"He stole your wand?!" Sylvie gasped.

Diana groaned. "Knowing a bit of magic *still* doesn't make me Lark Starling. Got it?"

"Got it," Sylvie agreed sheepishly.

"It *is* a good idea to keep that to yourself," Alban said. "I don't care, but to a lot of people out there, knowing *any* magic makes you a witch. And once they get that notion in their heads things will get...very ugly."

"Thank you for the warning," Diana said with a polite nod. "I do take your meaning, and that's exactly the point I was trying to make about introducing novelty. This a return visit for me, and I've encountered some of what you're talking about. Before anyone unleashes any more questions or concerns, though...Loki, would you please scout around and see if you can pick up Martin's trail?"

"Of course," the cat said, disappearing into the darkness almost before the words were out of his mouth.

"So, Mister Langridge, this concern that brought you here tonight was what exactly?" Diana asked.

"My legs," Sylvie answered for him.

"Umm...Yes. Something like that," Alban agreed.

"A concern as understandable as it is earthy," Diana said with a laugh that chipped away further at the formal demeanor she'd adopted. "Which reminds me...Excuse us a moment, won't you?" She pulled Sylvie aside several paces, then raised a hand adorned with a collection of rings that—at least for the most part—hadn't been there back at the convention. Diana slid a couple of them off her hand and presented both to Sylvie. "Enchanted," she said quietly. "The opal is supposed to keep you safe from any disease. So far it hasn't let me down. Haven't had a sick day since I started wearing mine."

"Seriously?" Sylvie gasped. "That's, like, priceless."

"Yeah. So don't go blabbing," she whispered. "They're not cheap or easy to make. But I owe you for coming to my rescue, and there's no telling what you've already been exposed to here. Also, it's supposed to keep you from being a carrier, so you don't infect the worlds you visit. We don't need to replay the whole bringing-plague-to-the-Americas thing. For everyone's sake, keep it on."

"And the...black one?" Sylvie asked. "Is that a pearl?"

"Black pearl, yes." Diana nodded. "A little insurance policy. It, uh...might take some more explaining."

"Wait.. Worlds I visit?" Sylvie whispered excitedly. "Like I can go to more?"

"That's sort of the plan, yes." Diana smiled. "Look, we'd better just take a walk so I can stop whispering." She pulled Diana back to the group. "Nami, will you be in charge of seeing that Mr. Langridge has legs to look at while I bring Sylvie up to speed?"

Manami laughed brightly. "Can do." It wasn't a hard assignment, Sylvie observed as she let Diana pull her away again, even as she felt a little twinge of jealousy at no longer having the man's undivided attention. Every hemline in sight was utterly scandalous by Victorian standards.

"Soooo...Where do I start?" Diana mused once they'd put a bit of distance between themselves and the others. "Big picture or immediate problems?"

"A little overview would be nice," Sylvie said.

"Fair enough," Diana said. "I was halfway through filming the *Lovelace* movies when I chanced on a journal nearly a hundred-and-fifty years old that had all sorts of rituals scribbled into it by one Molly Glass, a lady in a secret society devoted to magic and magical research. Long story short, I tried some of the simplest rituals out and met with enough success to keep me trying. By the time the last film was wrapping up I'd figured out enough to believe that the whole thing was genuine, but there were a lot of rituals I hadn't dared to try yet because they took more than one person. One in particular I was burning to find out about required a coven of five. Molly called it a 'narrative bridge'. It was supposed to open doors to fictional worlds. She mentioned personally visiting both Wonderland and Verne's 'Centre of the Earth'. I could barely contain myself but I was scared—very scared—of my friends deciding I was crazy.

"So I tricked Arthur and Felicity and Martin and Sonja into doing the ritual with me, pretending it was just a game as part of our farewell blowout. And it worked. We visited Lovelace. We *really* visited Lovelace. And we just got to explore because everybody thought we were our characters—until we started crossing paths with them, then it got really weird really fast, and everything spun out of control. It got scary when we realized everyone else could do real magic, but we still couldn't. We got out and decided that was an experience to never repeat, but we did start exploring other worlds. Loki followed me home from one of the first. We had to stay on our toes, yes, but all in all it was a great holiday...until we visited this one."

"Where...are we, exactly?" Sylvie asked.

"*Teprigoth*," Diana said. "Are you familiar with it?"

"Heard of it. Haven't read it. Steampunk, obviously. Also a bit of a haunted atmosphere, right?"

"Yeah. Magic and mystery beneath a veneer of steam-powered pseudo-science. And very urban. It all takes place in this one city. Anyway, we'd already been places that seemed a lot more dangerous, but this place is dangerous in its subtlety. We got caught up in a secret society here with promises of more magic. It turned out to be a cult. Again, long story short," Diana said, her voice beginning to break, "this place is the reason Arthur dropped off the grid. This is where he died."

"Oh no. I...I'm so sorry." That wasn't just polite sympathy. Sylvie had never met Arthur Allen, but if she'd had a bit of a thing for Martin as an actor, she'd totally crushed on Arthur's Isaac Rush as a character during her teen years. There'd been all sorts of tabloid speculation about his long silence, some of it morbid, but hearing straight from Diana that Arthur Allen was actually dead felt like a kick in the gut.

"We didn't dare take him home," Diana said. "You know, what if someone started asking where he was and actually found him? What if someone decided we'd been the ones to kill him? So you know where he's buried?" Sylvie didn't dare guess. She just waited Diana out. "Avalon. He's buried in Avalon."

"Damn, that's poetic," Sylvie said.

"He would have liked it," Diana said, wiping at her eyes with the back of her hand. "He earned it. Anyway..." She drew a long breath and took a few seconds to compose herself. "Anyway, the guys got it worse than the rest of us from the cult. Its leader...she called herself Bijou...turned out to be some sort of succubus thing. Maybe human, maybe used to be human, but seductive and manipulative and so dreamily fit, tossing around magics that Lark could only envy. She got her hooks deep into me and Felicity too, but she was more interested in the guys. We were under her spell for months before she over-played her hand with Arthur. She killed him for trying to get the rest of us to snap out of it, but killing him finished the job he'd started. We hightailed it for home."

"So Bijou..." Sylvie started.

"Gone. She's gone," Diana said fiercely. "We recruited Kassia back there into the coven—"

"The woman I hadn't met?"

Diana nodded. "Then we came back. We came back with a copy of Dante's *Inferno*."

It took a moment for that to sink in, then Sylvie's eyes began to widen. "So she's..."

"Yeah. She's. It was a lot harder than that makes it sound, but in the end it worked out and she's totally."

"I was told tonight how scary I am, but I yield the crown to you," Sylvie whistled. "No one crosses Lark Starling."

"No," Diana said, not even bothering to deny the name. "They don't." She took another long breath. "We came back more than a little messed up, though. Acting just felt so frivolous and pointless to me anymore. Same for Sonja, only worse. She's got some bad PTSD. Felicity did a decent job of bouncing back, but Martin...he's just been spiraling down ever since. I don't even know him anymore. He's been like an addict pining for his Bijou fix. Seems now he's convinced he can forge some of her old followers into a coven and rescue her by re-opening the bridge where we banished her."

"Can he?" Sylvie asked, worried.

"I don't know," Diana said. "Maybe. I'm not going to wait around and find out."

"Well, count me in for stopping him," Sylvie said. "No way I can walk away from this."

"No way?" Diana asked.

"I can't imagine one," Sylvie said. "I've been waiting all my life for magic like this. I can't just give up on it and spend my life thinking about what I missed."

"I've got one more caveat, then you can tell me that," Diana said. "Let's talk about the black pearl."

"Ookay," Sylvie agreed cautiously. "Let's talk about the black pearl. Is it cursed?"

"No," Diana said. "I told you it's insurance. Fictional worlds contain fictional characters. Fictional characters tend to be larger than life."

"This is true," Sylvie nodded.

"Have you kissed him yet?"

"Alban?" Sylvie could feel herself blushing. "Yeah..."

"How many men have you ever kissed within an hour of meeting them?" Diana asked.

"Ummm...One?" Sylvie said.

"One of the very first people you bump into in the very first fictional world you step into just happens to turn out to be one of the most handsome and intriguing men you've ever met?" Diana asked. "Practically intoxicating?"

Sylvie nodded guiltily.

"And he's more than passingly intrigued by your body," Diana asserted.

Sylvie nodded again. There was no arguing it even if there'd been a point.

"I don't have a complete grasp on the phenomenon, but there's been a lot of sexual energy in every world I've traveled to. It varies in degree and manifests differently place to place, but even in Wonderland the Queen of Hearts doesn't look a bit like the original illustrations. She's built like a '50s bombshell, and 'Off with her head!' rolls off her lips like a torch song. I promise that if you stick around every temptation you're already feeling is only going to re-double."

"That sounds...intense," Sylvie said.

"That pearl isn't really tested. I wouldn't put all my faith in it," Diana said. "But it's supposed to be birth control. Just in case everything else fails."

"Oh," Sylvie said. "So you haven't given into the temptation?"

"Of course I have." Diana laughed. "More than once. I just don't blindly trust magic to work as advertised when I have alternatives. I still get a flu shot every year even though you'll never catch me without the opal. Magic is great, but it can't beat science as a steady, reliable workhorse. When magic stops surprising you, it *becomes* science."

Sylvie slid the proffered rings onto her fingers, which were exposed by the fingerless gloves of her costume. "So to sum up:

magic is real, inter-dimensional travel is a thing, and these other worlds have lots of eye-candy?"

"It's more than just eye candy," Diana said. "They have spark. Electricity. It's like the whole world's giving off pheromones and you can't get away from them."

"I thought it was just me drunk on adventure," Sylvie said.

"Not just." Diana shook her head. "It's...Okay, let me back up a bit again. My invitation tonight, that was to try to recruit you for the coven. Nami made you sound like a really good fit and..."

"Wait." Sylvie held up her hand. "How long has Nami been in on this?"

"A couple of months," Diana said. "Don't derail me. Anyway, she's been lobbying to get you in the whole time. I like your resume. The point is you were supposed to show up, you'd get the interview, and—assuming all went well—we'd take you on a quick trip into a fun little steam-punk world so you wouldn't dismiss us as crazy. Then you'd get the recruitment spiel, this orientation, the caveats. Instead, Martin's waiting in the room when I show up, and we wind up here like this."

"One thing I'm still trying to figure out," Sylvie said. "The watchman back where we came in said he threw out the four of you—but there was no mention of Martin."

"Or of Loki I'd wager. The man was kind of preoccupied with four 'half-naked' women to keep an eye on," Diana said. "I think a marching band could've got by him unnoticed."

"Hang on," Sylvie said. "I just realized: this is the episode where everyone starts acting drunk and gets all touchy-feely, isn't it?"

"What?" Diana cocked an eyebrow.

"Metaphorically," Sylvie said apologetically. "This pheromone thing. This 'electricity'—it's kind of like that *Interstellar 2000* episode."

"I guess. In a way. If you squint at it right," Diana acknowledged with a grin. "I don't think it's some incidental effect, though. I think it's a carefully planned feature of the spell."

"What makes you think that?" Sylvie asked.

"Because passion and eroticism are big themes in the journal," Diana said, smiling wryly. "Yes, there are lot of nice, general-purpose rituals written down in there, but there's aphrodisiac potions and beauty spells, the birth-control thing, male performance enhancers, wardrobe-malfunction curses, self-enforcing magical 'safe words', an ex—"

"Got it," Sylvie interrupted.

Diana nodded. "Also, the secret society called itself the 'Sororital Order of the Freyjur'. I've done some research. They were ladies whose public raison d'être—as a group—was being cat fanciers, but *freyjur* is the plural of *freyja*."

"Like the Norse goddess?" Sylvie asked.

"Yes," Diana said. "It's also old Norse for 'lady'."

"And Freyja was associated with cats," Sylvie said. "*And* she was the Norse Aphrodite. A secret coven of high-born hedonistic witches masquerading as cat ladies. That's a bit clever, word-play wise."

"And I suspect they had many a secret tryst with their favorite fictional characters," Diana said. "I suspect that was the main point of developing the ritual. And rather than risk disappointment at the ritual's interpretation of Austen or Brontë, they made sure it defaulted to readings that were at least a bit naughty."

"Does it work with every book?" Sylvie asked.

"Every one we've tried. Also with films and role-playing settings, and even some short stories. Whether it conjures them into life or uses them as a reference to search through existing alternate universes looking for a match...who knows? But it transports us to settings within stories; not into the stories in progress themselves. There's no telling which part of the setting we'll wind up in, there's no telling where in the timeline we'll find ourselves, and nothing down that timeline after we arrive is fated to happen just because it was in our source material. Obviously, you can get a lot more precision out of using a stand-alone short story than a novel, but there seems to be some sort of minimum amount of setting detail needed for the spell to make sense of the request—so there's an absolute limit to the amount of precision you can get that way. Oh, and we've discovered that time keeps moving forward at a normal pace between visits."

"And you're inviting me to be a part of all this?" Sylvie asked.

"Yes," Diana said. "I'd say you passed the interview, you've got good character references, and you've got some very useful skills. I found the book, and I'm the main researcher. Felicity provides most of the funding since she's still raking it in as an actress. That makes us the senior partners, but we're choking off all the best possibilities if we aren't working in a coven of at least five. Like I said, I owe you for getting us out of there."

"Do you have a mission statement or anything?"

"After the original partnership dissolved, Felicity and I decided we wanted to revive the sorority and its study of magic," Diana said. "The name's too cheesy, of course. Too nineteenth-century. We're just calling ourselves the Freyjur."

"You're making a real-life *Lovelace*?" Sylvie asked excitedly.

"Pretty much," Diana agreed.

"I am *so* in," Sylvie said.

CHAPTER FOUR
THE MORNING-ISH AFTER

Sylvie found herself very reluctant to let go of sleep. The bed was soft and deliciously warm. Her dreams had been one exciting and erotic adventure after another, some of them still half-remembered. Despite her wishes, wakefulness came patiently stealing toward her, forcing her brain to gear up for the daily battle of separating fact from fantasy.

Today, the initial engagement—assembling a sensible time line of the previous days events—was proving a particular challenge. Had she been drinking? She must've. It wasn't a thing she did much of, especially not to excess, because she'd always felt cheated when she forgot having fun. She mercifully lacked any sort of hangover, but she was waking up in a bed that neither felt nor smelled like her own. The pillow she had her arm wrapped around was suspiciously warm, too, as was the quilt pressed up against her back. She could hear breathing that wasn't her own, feel two matching rhythms—one under her arm, the other behind her—and no memory could account for it. Had she *ever* shared a bed with two people? Maybe once or twice with Mom and Dad when she was four.

Yeah, she had to have been very drunk. Consciousness was about to arrive messy.

Resigned, she slowly opened her eyes to a mass of curly black hair. Suddenly she jerked upright, dislodging the hand that had been laying lightly on her hip and jostling the bodies that had sandwiched her. The jolt of adrenaline came less from the realization she was sharing a bed with a woman—okay, two women—and more from what it said about those dreams she'd been trying to make sense of. She stared back and forth between the two women as they shifted in their sleep, each of them assessing on some level whether now was the time that she should wake up.

Sylvie had just slept with Lark Starling and Holly Marsh together, like this was someone's erotic wish-fulfillment fan fiction. Well, okay, it was like erotic fan fiction would be without the nudity and such. At some point she'd traded out her steampunk corset for a convention t-shirt, and she was still in the bike shorts she'd been wearing under her skirt. Diana and Felicity were both in similarly improvised nightwear. Still, this was the kind of story that could turn Sylvie into a fan legend with even a full and faithful accounting of the facts.

She started to slide toward the foot of the bed, attempting to get up without waking either woman, then stopped herself midway and asked what she thought she was doing. Would she *ever* get another chance to cuddle up between the heroes of her school years, enjoying their warmth? Maybe, since she now had to re-evaluate some of those memories she'd dismissed as dreams, but only maybe. Right here, right now, for as long as her body and circumstance would permit, she was going to revel in the simple intimacy she'd been offered. She wriggled back into the position she'd woken up in. Diana and Felicity welcomed her back into the press of bodies. Sylvie sighed contentedly.

Taking advantage of the extra clues and the head-clearing jolt, Sylvie tried again at piecing together the narrative of how she'd gotten here. This time she ruled out alcohol. At least *some* of those unbelievable dreams had been real, and the time she'd lost could be put down purely to fatigue. Had she really stepped into another world last night? Had she really been walking around with a talking cat? As out-there as those two items seemed, they were intimately tied up in the most vivid and coherent string of memories she could pull together. Sylvie decided to cautiously trust that string until given reason to deny it.

The cat, then, had returned to their group after tracking Martin out of the park and into the all-night crowds of Teprigoth's entertainment district, where his scent had become impossible to follow. Sylvie had expected to launch immediately into some sort of search for him but Diana had surprised her by declaring they should start by returning to the hotel. Dewey had agreed readily enough, when approached respectfully, to let them in to return through the mysterious door in the attic.

Sylvie had then taken her leave to go looking for Brian, and that had turned into a total mess. He'd apparently babbled incoherently to security and to the police, who, after sending him off to the hospital, were in the process of studying security footage that made Sylvie the prime suspect as his attacker. It was nearly sunrise before that got cleared up, and the police went off to file the report that there'd been a drunken accident at a convention party—and no one was going to press any charges over it.

Word from Brian, now coherent, was that he'd be fine, and he insisted that Sylvie stay where she was and get some sleep rather than coming to see him. She promised him the full story as soon as it could be managed, and Felicity arranged a ride to pick him up whenever he was ready to leave the hospital. Then Sylvie had announced she was headed out to get some sleep.

When the limo got mentioned, Felicity had insisted Sylvie wasn't safe to drive. Sylvie had explained she wasn't going to drive, just to crash in the limo. In response, Felicity had insisted on getting Sylvie a room on-site, but it turned out there simply weren't any spaces to be had in the convention-packed hotel. Sylvie thought she remembered trying to say she'd be fine in the limo and Felicity dragging her away toward the elevators.

There, the thread of memories ended. For all Sylvie knew, she'd collapsed before reaching the elevators. She wondered if she'd managed to get out of the corset and into the t-shirt herself or if they'd had to manage it for her. Maybe Nami had helped since all the world was her locker room. Another key memory missing was why Sylvie was in this bed in particular. Even once she had been resigned to rooming with Diana for the night, this bed was hardly the only place in the suite she could have crashed. It was a huge king-sized bed, though, with plenty of room for three people who didn't mind getting close. The others must have been as exhausted as she was, and when sleep had become more important than sleeping arrangements they'd all just collapsed in the handiest space. In the absence of other information, that was the narrative Sylvie would stick with.

She managed a little more dozing before her body insisted she stumble to the bathroom. An alarm went off while she was still in there and she returned to find Diana and Felicity rousing themselves. By that time, the bedside clock claimed it was just after two in the afternoon.

"Hey, new girl," Diana greeted Sylvie with a sleepy smile from her perch on the edge of the bed. "Is your brain trying to pretend all that magic stuff was a dream?"

"Kind of, yeah," Sylvie admitted.

"It's not," Felicity assured her. "Well, anything about a polka-dotted dragon wearing tap shoes was a dream. The rest not so much."

"Does that mean it's time to go track down Martin?" Sylvie asked.

Diana shook her head. "Already on it. While you were asking after your friend last night, we did a little summoning ritual to find Loki some reinforcements. As we speak, there's a small cat army scouring Teprigoth to find him."

"Wait," Sylvie said. "I thought you had to have your book for the rituals."

"We do," Felicity said, rummaging in a drawer until she produced a red-cased electronic tablet that she tossed to Sylvie. "Here's your copy. It's just a partial for now—a beginner's guide."

Diana took it from there. "This isn't like one of those games where the writing itself is somehow special and magical. We made copies. We keep copies. The instructions are just really complicated and finicky. Trying to memorize them is like trying to memorize a gourmet cookbook written in a foreign language, then execute the recipes flawlessly. The problem isn't that I don't have access to my spells. The problem is that Martin does. He's got the password and everything. This is potent stuff, easily abused. Martin's come unhinged.

"Also, he's got the emergency copy that we layered protection enchantments onto and gave the magical equivalent of its own little cold fusion power source. It was supposed to be our emergency tool kit and ticket home when every other copy failed. That means it will be stupid expensive to replace and means it's going to stay usable in his hands for a long time. Letting him keep the book would be like letting a known terrorist wander off with a big cache of uranium and bio weapons."

"But you're trusting me with it?" Sylvie asked.

"With some of it for now," Diana said. "Keep even that bit safe. Keep it to yourself. The wi-fi has been gutted to make sure the tablet can't be infected or remotely hacked. Get with Kassia for your password. We'll go over full safety precautions and coven by-laws once we handle Martin.

"Now, I've got promises to keep to the convention. If you do too there's time to take care of that while we're waiting on Loki. Otherwise, just order room service on my tab and rest up to be ready."

With the costume contest still being hours away, Sylvie accepted the breakfast offer and—after venturing out to get her luggage—the use of a shower. By the time she was done, everyone seemed to have scattered to their various projects and commitments, leaving her alone in the suite with the door back to Teprigoth. Having surrendered the key she'd picked up to the suite, that left her with a choice. She could return to the convention not knowing when she'd be able to re-enter the suite, she could sit tight and try to decipher her new spell book, or she could go straight back across the bridge to another world. She loved the convention, but it was clearly the least option. She seriously considered taking a look at the tablet but decided there would be plenty of time for that later. Unlike the bridge, she wouldn't have to wait on the efforts of four other people to open it. Another world awaited.

Everything Sylvie had to wear on the expedition would be immodest by Victorian standards, so she opted to pull her costume back on as the choice that would be least glaringly out of place. Geared up for a few hours of light exploring, she ventured quietly back through the attic room and onto the landing beyond. No one appeared there to challenge her. The big house felt less spooky by the light of day but remained eerily quiet. Would Dewey be about somewhere? If he was, he might very well be sleeping. No one could be a one-man security detail twenty-four seven. Concerned that she might find herself breaking another innocent man's nose because Dewey had been replaced by the day shift, Sylvie descended the stairs as silently as she could manage until she arrived at the main floor. There she found Kassia, also in costume, curled up in sunbeam in a chair she'd uncovered, engrossed in reading a battered old book.

"*Hola, novata,*" Kassia greeted her, looking up. "How'd you sleep?" A mischievous glint in her eye suggested she'd seen the pile on the bed. Her accent wasn't strong, but it was there. Sylvie's untrained ear guessed the woman had grown up bilingual, either somewhere south of the border or somewhere near it.

"Deeply and contentedly but with weird dreams," Sylvie said, deciding on a non-evasive answer. It sounded like this whole endeavor was going to come with a side of emotional exposure. Pretending she hadn't enjoyed her night seemed pointless at best. "So Dewey's okay with us being here now?"

"Yeah. Seems he got nervous when some girl punched him in the nose and told him we were with 'The Convention'. *Please* don't let that be some sort of actual secret society," Kassia said, casting her eyes up prayerfully. "We swore we'd behave—stay quiet, don't take anything, don't break anything—and that he could keep looking at our legs. Speaking of which, be a dear and stick with the short skirts in here for the sake of keeping the peace." She smiled. "Also, your boy Alban promised him there'd be a job waiting if he got let go over us. He won't. This place used to be one of Bijou's, and he was hired by her solicitor to keep an eye on it after it was mothballed. Safe to say it's just gonna sit like this until she's declared legally dead. I think that'll be a few years yet. Don't know their laws."

"So what was your original 'in' with Diana and Felicity?" Sylvie asked, pulling the dust cover off another chair and curling up in it, facing Kassia across the sunbeam. "I hear you missed out on most of the Bijou episode. How did you meet?"

"After an award show for their last film," Kassia said. "I was a friend's plus-one that night. We wound up at the same party as Diana and her crew. Arthur tried to pick me up. I let him. We hit it off, exchanged numbers, I got invited to party with the crew a couple of times. Then they got caught up in this stuff and ghosted me. Next time I saw any of them it was Diana banging on my door with a talking cat to prove magic was real and beg me for help. That was right after Arthur died. She was a mess. I'm still behind the curve on the magic stuff, but I keep the coven up to speed on tech. I'm an engineer."

"Cool. So: you're the techie, Felicity's the money, Diana's the head witch...does Nami have a team niche yet?" Sylvie asked.

"She's the pretty one?" Kassia ventured with a grin.

Sylvie laughed. "You're *all* the pretty one."

"Why thank you." Kassia gave a pleased little smile. "Really, though, I guess she was brought on as our lust specialist."

Sylvie laughed again. "Seriously?"

"Yeah," Kassia nodded. "When we started talking last year about launching the Freyjur properly and getting our number back up to five, we agreed that we should try to get a better handle on *la química* and stop treating it as a window dressing."

"La kimmie-kuh?"

"The sexual chemistry always buzzing around on these worlds," Kassia said. "Diana did warn you about that? She likes to call it electricity. I call it *la química*. Same thing. Anyway, we decided that if three girls from Hollywood needed an expert on sexual chemistry the only place in the country left to turn was Vegas. I had my head down working on our spell book security, but Diana and Felicity flew out here and caught a lot of the acts—deep, serious research from the sound of it." She chuckled. "Nami's was apparently one of the best, and of every woman we took a closer look at she was easily the smartest and the most fun. One of the most empathic, too. Power without empathy should be a non-starter everywhere. It's like dumping a toaster in a bathtub. Anyway, it's fair to call her our lust expert."

"She's got no trouble making it pay the rent, that's for sure," Sylvie chuckled. "And where does that leave me? Diana said she liked my skills. She didn't say which skills she liked."

"You're the party's rogue, *novata*," Kassia grinned. "Nami showed us the vid of your parkour run down the strip. That's what got us back here. You're going to make it so much easier to explore. In seconds, you can get places that would send the rest of us scurrying to *maybe* find a spell that might possibly do something to eventually help us reach it. Bonus that it turns out you can deck an armed man when you need to."

"I got lucky," Sylvie demurred.

Kassia snorted. "Everything comes down to luck. The question is how good you are at loading the dice."

"Well, I haven't been caught at it yet," Alban said, appearing from behind Sylvie to casually perch on the arm of her chair. He'd abandoned the roguish costume and was now dressed as a proper Victorianish gentleman, complete with silver-tipped cane. He looked no less dashing for it.

"Hey!" Sylvie greeted him with a smile. "Didn't expect to find you hanging out here."

Alban shrugged. "Inherited wealth. I am a notorious man of leisure. That means everyone's given up on keeping track of how or where I spend my time and that I'd be deathly bored if I allowed myself to be. Besides, I promised you a roller coaster ride."

"Did you?" Sylvie asked. "I can't remember which of us promised who. Anyway, I'd love to." She turned her gaze back to Kassia. "Do you think there's time?"

"Yeah. Sure. We're *hedonistas*, remember?" Kassia smiled. "Go represent! And wherever Martin turns up it's bound to be on the far side of the park, so we'll be headed that way anyway. Just swing by the central fountain between rides so we can find you if we come looking. I think you'll need a costume change before hitting the street, though."

Sylvie cocked a questioning eyebrow at Alban.

"Leave it to me," he said, rising and offering his arm. Sylvie accepted it after a moment's hesitation. Kassia gave them a little farewell wave as they headed toward the back of the house.

"I thought you said I'd get to show off my legs," Sylvie said quietly.

"Did you want me to stop and explain that to her?" he asked, nodding back toward Kassia.

"Not particularly," she said.

"There you go then. But *I* thought *you* said something about riding naked."

"I did say *something* about it," Sylvie agreed. "You got me there. Where are we going if not to find me a proper dress?"

"You can't just walk down the street in that outfit," Alban said, "but I can get us to Poppikin through the back alleys if you're game."

"And *after* we get there?" Sylvie asked.

"Do you care?" He opened the door from a sitting room out into the back garden and led the way on out.

"What sort of question is that?"

The sun was up there somewhere, but even mid-afternoon the fog hadn't entirely burned off and the sky was overcast. Sylvie had heard that the famous "London fogs" had been largely pollution. That didn't seem to be the case here. The air was less oppressive than modern Vegas.

"What sort of *answer* is that?" He countered as they passed beneath the large old willow that dominated the garden.

"A sensible one?" she asked with an arched eyebrow.

"You see? That's the thing." He turned to her as they arrived at the gate.

"What's what thing?"

"Sensible doesn't ride roller coasters," he said, fixing her with a pointed gaze. "Sensible doesn't walk out of the house half-dressed in broad daylight. Not even with the idea of keeping to the back alleys. Even if she was fully dressed, *sensible* wouldn't wander down dark abandoned tunnels in the middle of the night with a man she'd just met."

"Wouldn't she?" Sylvie squeaked, her voice going small as she realized he was intruding on her personal space again, looming over her.

"*Nothing* you did last night was built on a foundation of sensible. And if I want sensible, I have a whole city full of women just waiting to give it to me. Neither one of us is here for the sensible." His face hovered inches from hers again as Sylvie realized he'd backed her up against the gate. A part of her was taking stock of where the various bits of her arsenal were strapped on in relation to her hands, assuring herself she'd not forgot them in getting dressed after that odd and exhausting night. "If you really regret teasing what you might do for one kiss, I'm going about this all wrong and we should find you that dress." He stepped back, releasing her personal space, and waited for her to react.

She offered him an apologetic little smile. "Sorry. I guess I did go a bit hot-and-cold on you. I'm brand new to this world-hopping thing and Diana hit me with some facts of life last night. The short version is I was a little bit drunk when we met, and I'll be a little bit drunk whenever I'm here. Not *literally* drunk, but I'm going to be less clear-headed, more impulsive than I'm used to. On the one hand: fun! On the other hand: I don't know how far to trust myself. Expect me to act a bit weird."

"Okay." Alban gave a little nod. "That makes sense. I mean your reaction make sense, not the being not-literally drunk. That part...I guess is just a thing. Reality doesn't have to make sense, does it?"

"Not in my experience," Sylvie agreed. "It just says, 'Jump.' We say, 'How high?'. It says, 'Guess...'"

Alban gave a hearty laugh. "I like that summary, yes. But if you can't trust your own judgment, I can't trust *my* judgment where it comes to you. That'll leave us both acting weird. It might be better if I step back and let you figure things out—let you come find me when you 'sober up'."

"I *did* sober up," Sylvie said. "I had my talk with Diana. I went home. I did all sorts of unpleasant adulting. I crawled into bed and slept myself out. I had a good breakfast. I weighed my options. Then I came running back here hoping I could spend some more time a little bit drunk with you. Please don't go away, and please don't stop flirting with me. It's fun and I don't meet a lot of guys who do it well. I'm just going to be a bit...weird."

He nodded acquiescently. "All right then. Did sober you still want to show off her legs?"

It was Sylvie's turn to laugh. "Yes! Absolutely!"

It was nice feeling naughty about a thing she'd gone her whole life simply not thinking about. It was nicer how sexy it made her feel that it riveted the attention of a man like Alban. Sylvie was definitely going to have to visit more worlds where modern fashion would be considered unspeakably risqué. It evoked such a heady emotional combination of forbidden thrill and secure confidence.

Back home, while her costume was meant to be sexy it was only "night on the town" sexy. Had she been out on the open street in it here she'd no doubt it would be causing old women to conjure up fainting spells and young men's jaws to drop. That added a feeling of edgy danger even to walking the back alleys. Though those remained quiet, at any moment someone might round a blind corner, step out of a gate or doorway, or even just look out a window and be treated to an unobstructed view of her brazen wickedness. Neither she nor Alban actually expected her to reach Poppikin Park completely unseen. What the route did do was keep the level of possible exposure down to a manageable limit.

They'd made it about five blocks before the first set of new eyes found her. Almost disappointingly, those eyes belonged to a cat. The cat darted quickly away but not, Sylvie guessed, out of any alarm at the length of her skirt. She wondered if it had been one of the cats out looking for Martin.

Their next encounter was with another street-sweeping robot. It so completely filled the alley that they had to press themselves back into a recessed doorway to let it clank past. Again, it offered no commentary on her skirt.

Halfway to the park, Sylvie was starting to feel a little vexed at the lack of attention, when she finally caught someone's middle-aged manservant staring at her from out of a second-story window with a gratifyingly slack jaw. She paused and smiled up at him with a little wave, then took her skirt in both hands and hoisted the hemline another inch as she turned this way and that, posing for him. The man met the display with a grin and a wink as he silently clapped his hands in a show of approval. Sylvie blew him a kiss and dropped a curtsy before turning and heading off to catch up with Alban, who hadn't broken stride.

Wow. This was so much more fun than dealing with the way men acted back home. The ladies who came up with this sensually charged spell certainly knew what they'd been doing. It was also reassuring to have an explanation why she'd yet to meet a man here who simply acted like a desperate, clueless jerk. It gave her real hope that what she was seeing would continue as the norm, not the exception. They ran out of alley before running into anyone else, but that one good moment of appreciation buoyed Sylvie, completely erasing the feeling of disappointment that had been creeping up on her.

"Now what?" she asked as they peered out around the corner at the main gates of the park. A steady stream of locals from various walks of life strolled in and out—too many for her to have any hope of slipping past unnoticed.

"Now you wait patiently out of sight," Alban said. "I'll be back as quickly as I can."

Sylvie nodded her acceptance and watched him cross the street to merge with the crowd and disappear through the gates. She waited and watched for a couple more minutes before realizing she wasn't exactly out of sight here—and that her corset didn't blend with the outerwear of the women on the street any more than her miniskirt did. She was already attracting too much attention even if the people who'd seen her so far had been far enough away to doubt what they were seeing as she leaned out of the alleyway. Sylvie beat a hasty retreat and settled down behind a rain barrel, where she pulled out her phone again to kill some time. She'd fired up her web browser before realizing how ridiculous the thought was. Of course, her phone failed to find a signal. For a plan B, she opened up the rogue-like dungeon crawl game that served as her current time waster and worked through a couple of levels before Alban returned.

"Here we go," he said, holding up a full-length coat. "I think this will fit reasonably well."

"The old 'sneak a girl past in just her lingerie under a coat' gambit." Sylvie chuckled. "Classic. Where'd you get it?"

"Belongs to a friend," he said. "You'll still attract some stares. The coat's overkill for this weather. No one will be forward enough to call you on it though."

"That'll do," Sylvie said, accepting the coat and slipping into it. "At least for making an entrance. Is that the whole plan—me walking around in a coat? I guess I can unbutton it on the roller coaster."

"Honestly, I can't get the image out of my head of you strolling up to the coaster starkers beside me and riding that way," Alban said with a grin. "Come on."

Sylvie laughed but accepted his arm and headed across the plaza with him toward the gates. "What are the laws on that even?" she asked. "There's a big difference between breaking laws and just violating social taboo."

"Strictly illegal," Alban assured her. "You'd never get out of the park without being arrested. Unless..."

She elbowed him in the ribs. "One more dramatic pause and I'm not even going to hear you out. Keep it moving."

"Unless you get your timing right," he finished.

"The fact I'm even curious what that timing would be makes me doubt my judgment," Sylvie said. "Let's stop at the scandalous legs."

"Then just pardon me undressing you with my eyes," he said.

"I'll be very disappointed if you don't."

They strolled together through the gates and into the old carnival atmosphere of Poppikin Park. The reality of the place alive with crowds did look quite a bit like Sylvie's midnight imaginings, if more rough around the edges. The crowds were both thicker and less genteel, ranging from the threadbare lower end of the middle class to its polished and posturing upper end that aspired to become something more while not quite being ready to give up on the simple pleasure that came with remaining below the aristocratic stratosphere. Perhaps a few were actual upper-class folk brazen enough to be unafraid of getting caught slumming it, but if so those remained scattered and indistinguishable from the families of wealthy businessmen. The occasional service robot would also clank past, disrupting the pseudo-historic nostalgia of it all.

The eye-catching centerpiece of the park was its towering Ferris wheel. It was twice the height of any Sylvie had personally seen before and with enclosed gondolas large enough to hold at least eight passengers, the whole thing painted in bright primary colors. She'd seen the silhouette of it last night, but been unable to appreciate its size for want of a visual frame of reference. In the shadow of the Ferris wheel, a multi-tiered fountain stood in the middle of the plaza, its metal sculptures an oxidized green. Though the fountain was dwarfed by the Ferris wheel, the pipe-playing, Pan-like figure crowning it sat on a sculpted stump that had been elevated no less than twenty feet into the air.

The curved outer wall of the park drew Sylvie's eye next. Again, there had been no way to appreciate it in the night. The entire wall had been done up in a sophisticated, colorful mosaic of an alpine landscape realistic enough that she could almost feel the depth of the receding layers of mountains. Various bits of actual, three-dimensional landscape jutted out from the wall, enhancing the effect, and through it all wound the roller coaster that had instantly caught her fancy. By the light of day, she could see the tracks winding through artificial tunnels and over carefully sculpted hills. Carloads of excited thrill seekers made the journey on its track around the perimeter of the park with all the break-neck speed of a kiddie coaster, but that didn't dampen her enthusiasm for the artistry of it or for the fact that it wasn't even on Earth.

"Oh, wow," she marveled as they passed a carousel filling the air with its festive siren song. "I've never seen one like that."

"I think there's two or three scattered around the city," Alban said, "but yeah, they're pretty rare." He stood and contentedly studied her enthralled face as she watched the horses climb and dive around a course of irregular hills.

"Please tell me they come to life and take off across country," Sylvie begged.

"Maybe," Alban said. "If you ride them bareback."

She met his mischievous grin with a wry smile. "You do have a one-track mind, don't you?"

"Yeah," he admitted. "But it's only because the scenery is to die for."

Sylvie chuckled. "Kissing you would be scandalous here wouldn't it?"

"Pretty much," he agreed. "That's what the canal tour is for." He gestured off toward a point in the outer wall where people were queuing for a parade of small, four-passenger boats that floated in and out through dark archways. Most of the boats seemed to leave the dock only half-filled.

"Is that a 'tunnel of love'?" Sylvie asked, intrigued.

"If by that you mean 'polite excuse for couples to have a little time alone in the dark', yes."

"All right. Let's add that to the short list." Sylvie giggled. "I want to ride absolutely everything and just realized I have no money at all they'll accept. They'll expect money, won't they?"

"They'll expect money," Alban agreed. "I've got it covered."

She flashed him a smile. "Thank you. You know yesterday was the first time I ever saw real magic, ever stepped outside my own world, ever met someone from another world. This park may not be overtly magical. I've been to places like this that were bigger, faster, more showy. Maybe your robots are ahead of ours. Not much else is. But this is still something hardly anyone from back home has ever seen, and maybe not one of them has ever ridden these things. I want so much right now to be the first girl ever to ride a roller coaster on another world. Is that stupid?"

"No." He led her aside to where a bucket of colored chalk had been left by a sidewalk art gallery. "Look," he said, grabbing up a piece and kneeling to draw a short, curved line on the sidewalk. "Does that mean anything to you?" he asked, pointing to it.

Sylvie shook her head. "Not to me, no."

"How about this?" He drew another curved line turned sideways to the first, followed by a straight line that angled off to the side.

"Still no. Is it a code?" She asked.

"Yes." He went down his row of lines, adding a bit to each, turning the first into a hook, the second into a circle, and the third into a forked line.

"'Joy?'" Sylvie read.

Alban nodded. "Now see that mountain scape?" he asked, pointing to the outer wall of the park as he got back to his feet. "If you walk up to stand six inches from it, all you'll see is a jumble of colored tiles. Even a masterwork painting is made up of meaningless brush strokes. The greatest works of philosophy, of science, of literature are all made up of sentences that are made up of words that are made up of letters that are made up of arbitrary lines. We can get reductionist on anything and everything until it seems reduced to pointlessness. Meaning can only come from context. Never apologize for your joys just because you doubt they're profound. Joy is one of the most important building blocks we have to work with."

Sylvie smiled as he took her arm again. "So are you just a dilettante philosopher, or is it some sort of calling? You haven't told me yet what it is you do when you're not attending *those* kinds of parties."

"Hmmm..." Alban pondered. "Do you want a straight answer or the amusing one I give everybody else?"

"Both?" Sylvie suggested.

"Drat." Alban sighed. "Now I've corned myself into proving I'm amusing. Plus, you caught me in the lie that I tell everyone the same story. I never can keep it straight. All right. Stop me if you've heard this one: I'm a professional wombat trainer."

"I'll admit to a mild amusement." Sylvie smirked. "Is there any hint of truth to the story?"

"I've never seen a wombat in my life," Alban admitted, "but if we stop by the zoological garden I can show you the empty pen that still has a plaque on it that says 'wombat'. I don't think that counts as a hint of truth, but perhaps you'll allow it as a vague allusion to something which is not entirely false?"

"I'll allow it." Sylvie grinned. "Now what about the straight answer, and why I would rate one? My legs aren't *that* special."

"For those answers I'll insist you accompany me on a canal tour," he said.

"The price of truth is a make-out session?" She cocked an eyebrow.

"The price of truth is privacy," Alban said. "Anything else we used the privacy for would be a bonus."

Sylvie shrugged. "I do want to ride everything, so no harm starting there."

CHAPTER FIVE
THE MINISTRY OF MISBEHAVIOR

The first thing Sylvie used their privacy for as they floated away into the dark tunnel was to shrug off the coat and kick her feet up onto the rail in front of their bench, offering up as a good a view to her appreciative audience as the light would allow. For now, there was nothing else to see. "So," she said, "that straight answer?"

Alban held out a hand to her. She accepted it and leaned comfortably into his shoulder. "First," he said, "I offer this as a secret for a secret. I'm keeping yours, I'm expecting you to keep mine. Fair?"

"Totally," she agreed.

"I'm something of an outlaw," he said. "A political subversive. The pay's not good, but like I said, I'm not hurting for money. I *was* hurting for purpose until I realized how many people around me are routinely victimized in a city where the people in power are more concerned with what's proper than with what's right."

Sylvie giggled before smiling apologetically. "Sorry. It just sounds so much like a superhero origin story when you say it that way," she said. "I get what you mean, though. And I guess it even makes sense it would sound that way."

"Good to hear some part of that makes sense to one of us," Alban said.

"Yeah. I need to remember not to overtax whatever's translating for us with too much modern idiom," Sylvie said. "But basically, Diana said they used a storybook as a navigation guide to bring us here. I was saying you sound like one of our fictional archetypes, but that's probably because the spell was looking for people who would."

"Interesting," Alban said. "I hope it thinks I'm one of the good guys."

"So far I'm thinking 'yes'," Sylvie said, giving his hand a squeeze. "So there was no costume party? You were just sneaking around at night in a mask?"

"There was no costume party," Alban confirmed. "Someone saw your friends being threatened by your...*not* friend? The one with the gun. Anyway, I was there looking into it. Since my contact had taken them for ladies of the evening, we both knew the constables wouldn't bother themselves about it."

"Are you saying I'm dressed like a prostitute?" Sylvie asked without rancor.

"Maybe like a really successful one who knows she doesn't have to try too hard," Alban suggested.

"I guess I can live with that," she said. Up ahead, flickering gaslight appeared from around a bend in the tunnel, hinting they were done with the initial plunge into darkness and would be getting some sort of actual tour soon.

"And you're saying that to you I'm a fictional character?" Alban asked.

"Like one, sort of," Sylvie said. "None of us seem to know exactly how it works. Anyway, Diana was clear that even if you're in the story you're not locked into following it. At a *minimum* you started out as an idea in someone's head and now you have a life of your own. I want to think it's like what I said, though, where an infinite number of realities already exist, and we just got pointed to one that looks like the book. I've never read the book myself. You might not be in it at all—or you might just wander briefly through."

They floated past an innocuous, three-dimensional set piece of dockside city life with sophisticated animatronics. A dog growled softly at a cat who hissed back at it from atop a crate. Worker robots with mannequin-like features continually loaded and unloaded prop cargo from a barge as the little boat floated past it. The facade of a cathedral—probably meant to be the one with the silhouette Sylvie had followed last night—rose above the scene in the background.

"But you already compared me to a hero," Alban observed wryly. "I don't think it's safe to assume I can keep secrets from you. It sounds like dangerously good odds you've got a melodramatic version of my biography waiting for you at home."

"And what would it tell me about you if I did?" Sylvie asked.

The dock scene disappeared around the bend behind them. A glimmer ahead promised more set pieces to come.

"It'd paint me as a womanizer to start, not a romantic lead," he said. "That's probably the first thing you need to know."

"Well that's a relief." Sylvie giggled. "If it made you out as a romantic lead I'd be stomping all over someone else's happily ever after here, wouldn't I?"

"That...is a seriously good point," Alban agreed.

"And you do know that the bad boy who can only be tamed by the 'right' woman is one of the most enduring romance-novel fantasies?" Sylvie said. "Calling yourself a womanizer just ups the chances you were written to be reformed."

"There's no way to win this one, is there?" he asked as they floated serenely past a street-festival scene.

"None. But don't worry," she said. "I totally see you as a lust object with benefits. Any other confessions?"

"I never fight fair, and I'm completely ruthless when I have to be," Alban said. "I think anything else can wait."

"Still not discouraged from making out with you," Sylvie said.

"These benches aren't actually that great for it despite their reputation," he said.

"Experience speaking?"

"Yes." At that, he reached for the cane he'd left leaning against the forward rail and used it to swat at a dangling sign as they passed under it. Painted with a bottle of wine, a round of cheese, and a bunch of grapes, the sign bore the name "Fena Rosada" in a showy font, none of which offered a clue why he might choose to offer it such abuse.

"What was that about?" Sylvie asked.

"A better option than the bench."

The boat passed once more into darkness, then indistinct noises from up ahead slowly resolved themselves into the strains of a lively orchestra accompanied by voices raised in song. One more bend in the tunnel brought them up to a street scene centered around a decent mock-up of a grand, marble-columned building adorned with classical statues that put Sylvie in mind of the Greek muses. Music and laughter spilled out of the gold-painted doors with the tinny overtones of a primitive speaker system. Stiff silhouettes whirled across the shades in the windows to suggest the presence of dancers. The boat stopped directly in front of the facade with a gentle bump. Alban immediately hopped out and offered Sylvie a hand after him. "Come on," he said. "The next boat's never far behind."

"What? You've got a bed stashed back here?" she laughed.

"Now there's an idea..." He grinned at her mischievously. "Maybe next time. Come on."

"We *are* going to finish the tour, right?" she asked as she allowed herself to be pulled up beside him.

"Rogue's honor," he swore with a hand to his heart as he kicked at a small metal plate on the floor. The current caught the boat again, and it started to drift away. "We can walk out of here when we need to," he said without waiting for another question. "There's maintenance access to all the set pieces."

"Mmmm...Making out behind the bleachers," Sylvie purred. "I haven't done that since...No, wait. I never made out behind the bleachers. That was some girl in one of those teen dramas. I keep mixing me up with fictional characters. I guess that's only going to get worse now."

Alban laughed as he dragged her into a large nook sheltered behind the edge of the facade with an old wooden door at the back. "You strike me more as the type to make out in front of the bleachers anyway."

Sylvie giggled. "Just the once. For about two weeks in high school I had a boyfriend who played baseball and we were rather...indiscreet."

"I know neither what makes a school high nor what makes a ball base, but I applaud your indiscretion," Alban said as he took her hand in his, dropped the other to her waist, and began gently spinning her around their concealed little space to the music coming over the speakers. "We have entirely too much discretion around here, and I'd hate for you to bring us more."

"Hey! I know this one," Sylvie said as she began singing along with the recorded voices. "I'm half crazy," she sang, "all for the love of you." After half a verse she stopped. "That's so weird you have one of the same songs we do. It's quite old, but it's definitely ours."

"It's new here—at least in this part of town. Can't be much more than a year ago I started hearing it. Very catchy though."

"Must be cross-contamination between our worlds," Sylvie said. "I'll bet one of my friends taught it to a pub crowd or something last time they were here." The song had actually served as a *Lovelace* plot point by virtue of being played on a music box that Lark's great-great-grandmother had left her, and that, of course, turned out to be a crucial clue to unlocking family mysteries. Any or all of the cast could have picked up an affinity for the song on set, but that only supported her larger theory.

"Must have," Alban agreed. Catching Sylvie's coat as he spun her away, he'd smoothly slipped it off of her almost before she realized what he was doing. She laughed as he folded it neatly and laid it atop a crate that could either have been a prop or an authentic box of supplies. Smiling, Sylvie struck a pose with one bare leg forward for his review. He blew her one of those continental kisses she'd seen chefs in old movies use to declare something delicious. She giggled again, then started to speak—but Alban held up a finger to his lips and nodded out toward the canal. When she paused she could hear the sounds of quiet conversation approaching. He moved in close and pulled her into the dance again.

"Laugh. Dance. Sing along," he murmured. "As long as you're out of sight, any passerby will take it for part of the tour. But we might want to keep the banter to a whisper here."

Sylvie tilted her head to smile up at him again, and he leaned in to kiss her. It wasn't a rushed kiss, but there was nothing tentative about it this time. The dance faltered as the kiss drew out, his tongue teasing across her lips, her lips parting to let it in. A couple of steps backward to keep her balance brought her up against the wall, with Alban following right along and right back into the kiss. She clutched at him as his lips trailed over her cheek and down her throat to linger on her breast bone, exposed by her corset along with the cleavage.

They were both breathing hard by the time he straightened up, and she saw she'd left a lipstick mark on his forehead as he'd started his way down. She let out a happy little giggle as a mental picture of him as one of those cartoon characters stumbling dazedly away from an off-screen interlude covered with perfect little lip prints flashed across her mind. She'd never gone in for makeup much, except when she was in costume, and she'd never much mixed costuming and dating. She'd only put it on this afternoon out of costuming habit. This was probably the most distinct lipstick smudge she'd ever left. It seemed right for the moment.

"I *do* know where there's a love seat back here," Alban said. Sylvie responded with a quick but distinct nod. He led the way, but to her surprise he ignored the door beside them, instead peering around the corner of the facade to make sure they were between boats. Taking her by the hand and dodging animatronic figures, he pulled her around to the gold-painted front doors of the facade and delivered them a sharp series of raps.

After a moment Sylvie heard the sliding of a bolt, and then the doors swung slowly open, guided by another mannequin-like figure dressed up in a red usher's uniform. Behind that primitive android lay a broad tunnel floored in gold-veined black marble and lined with mirrors that reflected back and forth between each other into infinity. Five electrically lit crystal chandeliers dangled from the fifteen-foot ceiling, evenly spaced down the length of the tunnel. The tunnel descended two short flights of stairs before ending at a pair of ornate, gilded double doors that could have been the original model for the cheap tourist mock-up they'd just stepped through.

"What is this place?" Sylvie asked. The mirrors confronted her with endless reflections of herself in her little look-at-me, faux-Victorian costume and left her feeling suddenly even more under-dressed than if she'd walked back out into the crowded park like this. "And shouldn't we go back for the coat?"

"Do you *want* the coat?" Alban asked. "No one to miss it here but you."

"I...Yeah. I mean no. Leave it," she giggled. She was getting *very* giggly, she noticed, losing what remained of her inhibitions and her social filters. She had no specific memory of acting like this when she was drunk, but she'd definitely caught herself acting like this when she was sleep-deprived. "Wait. Hang on," she said, holding up a restraining finger. She walked to the first flight of stairs down, descended it in quick, nimble steps, then turned around and returned up it just as quickly. There was no uncertainty to her step, no sluggishness or lack of balance. That was comforting at least. "We are *definitely* in that episode," she announced.

"Again, I don't know what that means," Alban said.

"It means you're my designated driver," she said, shoving a finger at his chest. "It means I'm going home unless you swear to keep me from doing anything monumentally stupid."

"I do monumentally stupid stuff all the time," he said, "even when I'm stone-cold sober."

"You know what I mean," she insisted.

"No," he said. "I don't. I can't swear to something that vague. Your stupid and my stupid may be two different things."

"I'm not allowed to make any life-altering decisions," she said. "No tattoos. No frivolous gambles with life, limb, or health. No risking my chance to go home. No making promises or signing contracts. No joining the foreign legion. No joining cults. *These,*" she said, waggling her fingers with the rings Diana had given her, "never come off for anything. They're for keeping everybody safe. If I say no to anything, that's my final answer. I don't just mean 'don't badger'. I mean I don't get to waffle or change my mind later. Not until I get home and clear my head.

"And no risking children," Alban said. "Got it."

"I'm sure as I can be that's not a risk or I wouldn't have trusted myself to come back," Sylvie said. "That one's on me. Swear to me about the other stuff."

"And if I have to tie you up and drag you home to stop you?"

"Do it," she said.

"Okay," he said. "I'll do it."

"Swear?"

"I swear," he said. "Relax and enjoy. I'll get you home in one piece, physically and emotionally."

"Okay then," Sylvie said, mollified, and allowed herself to be led down the tunnel as the usher-bot swung the doors closed behind them. "So what is this place?" she repeated her earlier question as they arrived at the inner doors.

"This," Alban said, pushing them open, "is the Grand Imp Music Hall."

What it looked like was a spacious old theater lobby, echoing and empty, all marble, mirrors, red velvet curtains, gilt appointments, and crystal chandeliers. As Sylvie stood soaking it in, the doors shut behind them, locking out another tinny chorus of Bicycle Built for Two. "'Imp' as in 'Imperial'?" she asked, still craning to take it all in.

"'Imp' as in 'Impish'," Alban said. "As in indulgence and indiscretion. Speaking of which, did you want to claim the love seat behind the bleachers or the love seat in front of them?"

"Which is which?" Sylvie laughed.

"Behind the bleachers." Alban pointed toward a secluded alcove in one corner, set off with a beaded curtain. "In front of the bleachers." He pointed toward a door out one side of the grand room.

"You're not going to tell me where it goes, are you?" she asked.

"Of course not," he agreed.

"Come on then," she said, heading off toward the door. "You know I'm curious. Just don't think I'm making any sort of commitment without knowing what I'm getting into."

"I wouldn't let you," Alban said. "I'm the discontinued driver, remember?" Arriving just ahead of her he opened the door and ushered her into a small, brick-walled sitting room with a few couches and stuffed chairs arranged around a central table laid out as for a game of poker. A single door on the far side offered the only other way out. An overhead electric lamp offered the only light. "We're mostly just passing through," he assured her. "This is only an invitation to strip poker if you want it to be." She smirked in response. "But we should still pause long enough to observe tradition." He pointed her toward a chair at the table and grabbed one opposite her before picking up a single chip from beside him and tossing it into the middle of the table. With a nod he encouraged her to do likewise. She did. He shuffled the deck, cut it, and proceeded to deal them each a card. "High card wins both chips. Is it a bet?"

"Just the chips?" she asked.

"Yes."

"Just two chips? Belonging...to somebody else?"

"They're sort of community property," he said. "But yes. It's a tradition."

Sylvie shrugged. "Sure." She flipped over the queen of hearts and gave him an amused but accusing look.

"I promise that wasn't planned," he laughed, holding up his hands defensively before flipping over the five of spades. "Your chips." She gathered them onto the pile beside her. He tossed out another chip. "Again."

Ten hands later, she was laughing at the absurdity of it all as he surveyed his dwindling pile of chips. "How long is this supposed to go on?" she asked.

"Until I finally win one," he said, rolling his eyes. When he at last was able to show a queen to her ten, he gathered up the two chips onto his pile and stood. "Good. *Now* we can go on," he said.

"What was that all about then?" she asked as he led the way to the other door.

"Our alibi," he said, stepping into the brickwork tunnel beyond the door. "I can now honestly and with conviction announce I've lost a bet to you. You can say you've lost one to me. And how much insane behavior in the history of...well, I suppose now I should say the multiverse...do you think has been explained away with the simple declaration, 'I lost a bet'? So long as one fails to disclose the terms of the wager, one's audience will jump to the obvious conclusion."

Sylvie laughed. "This does not bode well," she said, but she was smiling.

They climbed a stairway back up and then continued along the dimly lit corridor as it twisted and turned past a succession of doors. As they approached the third door, it opened abruptly, and a pretty, brown-haired woman in a bright blue dress stepped out.

"You said there was no one here!" Sylvie hissed urgently, but that was all the conversation there was time for before the woman finished latching the door and looked up to see them.

"Hey, Alban," she smiled. "Who's your friend?"

"Ettie, this is Sylvie," Alban said.

"Pleasure to meet you, Sylvie," Ettie said, eying her outfit. "Love the look. It suits you."

"Oh, umm...Thank you," Sylvie said, relaxing. It was kind of strange remembering that covering up had never been her idea in the first place.

"I guess you were the one needing my coat though."

"Yeah," Sylvie admitted, biting her lip while unsuccessfully fighting back a guilty little smile. "That was me."

"Sylvie was mentioning something last night about liking to wear even less," Alban said with a grin.

"Well that'd be something," Ettie laughed. "I'll bet you look amazing in less too." She flashed Sylvie a smile.

Sylvie felt a dizzying warmth gather in her chest and rise toward her head at the compliment. "It's okay then? I really thought there was no one else here."

"Wear as little or as much as you like," Ettie said. "It's okay. And in this case, I think we can call it a public service. That outfit is *tres* cute. I've got to run, though. That ripper from Murkwell is sniffing around the park again."

"Did you want some backup?" Alban asked.

"I'm the backup, thanks," Ettie said. "I was just gathering up to go help. You two have fun. It was nice meeting you, Sylvie. See you soon I hope." With that she was off, striding purposefully down the corridor.

"I said that there was no one to miss your coat," Alban said quietly as Ettie disappeared around a corner. "I promise she doesn't miss it."

"What's a ripper?" Sylvie asked, deciding to let him have that one. It helped she was pleased to unjustifiable levels to have been discovered like this and then given such a warm reception.

"Someone who should be a criminal but isn't," Alban said. "Either because the law was built to protect them or because it was built to work against their victims."

"So...this is that 'Ministry of Misbehavior', yes?" she said. "And you're part of it?"

Alban nodded. "We were a little social club with a tongue-in-cheek name and a lot of money, carving out a sanctuary. The city can be unforgiving. We got into politics when an alderman tried to shut us down as part of a 'public morals' campaign. We blackmailed him. It's amazing how often the self-appointed guardians of morality in the world are up to their necks in corruption. So he ended the crusade, declared victory by shutting down our old meeting hall with our blessing, and helps keep our new sanctuary here free from official scrutiny. Over the last couple of years we've gained enough allies, both willing and grudging, to become a sort of shadow government for this ward of the city. We keep to our lane—providing an outlet for victimless crimes and policing the predatory behavior that would get overlooked without us—and the public powers maintain a polite fiction that we don't exist."

"All of which means I really don't have to worry about a dress code in here? Or to reign in the public displays of affection?"

"Right," Alban agreed, smiling. "And in two or three hours the park is going to close to the public and host a private event, like it does every night. This being Saturday, it'll be for the Ministry and its guests."

"Meaning there will be no dress code out there either?" Sylvie hazarded a guess.

"None."

"I *could* literally stroll up naked to the roller coaster for you and they'd welcome us on board?" The heat that had spread upward from her chest lanced suddenly down through her stomach and kept right on past.

"The roller coaster. The Ferris wheel," he said. "The fun house. The carousel..."

"Has anyone actually done that sort of thing?" Her head was buzzing. Her heart rate had jumped enough for her to feel the pounding. From the light in his eyes as he brushed her hair back from her face, he could have been hearing the pounding of her heart too.

"I think a few of the ladies are building up to it," Alban said. "Strolling the grounds in corset and petticoats has become a fashion. But starkers? No one's gotten quite that brave yet."

"I could be the first?" She sounded breathless even to herself. Her mouth had gone dry.

"Yes," he said, his fingertips tickling lightly across her cheek. Sylvie's field of vision seemed to narrow until nothing existed but his eyes. She could practically feel herself falling into them. "If that's what you want, Sylvie," he said. "What do you want?"

"I, uh...I think I want to sit down," she managed. "You said there's a love seat?"

So much for steady and sure-footed, Sylvie thought as she stumbled along, leaning against Alban while she tried to walk her body through the simple mechanical steps of breathing. Inside she could feel her id—the one that had always contented itself with dressing provocatively and fishing for admiration—rage to be let out into this promised, perfect storm of fully sanctioned naughtiness that would remain far more secret than anything that happened out in Vegas.

Some part of her was aware that in the physical world they'd passed through a door, then she was sitting with her head between her knees, trying to coax the world to stop spinning.

"Are you all right?" His concerned voice sounded distant, echoing. "Should I get you a physician?"

"Just...give me a minute," she managed. If this was *la química* off the chain, then "intense" didn't begin to describe it. Or was this purely her own mind and body, giddy with the freedom to acknowledge desires she'd kept haphazardly suppressed? Either way, every awkward dream she'd ever had about realizing she was naked in class or, more recently, in the front of her limo while ferrying a client, had come rushing back at once with all the adrenaline but with zero sense of the shame. The dreams hadn't returned alone, either. Her mind also danced with dozens of recurring fantasies and real memories in which her exposed flesh played a welcome starring role as someone's object of lust.

Breathe, she reminded herself. *Breathe.*

There was sound. She focused on the sound. Someone was crooning a song Sylvie didn't know. The sound crackled and hissed, probably spilling out from the horn of a gramophone. It was a nice song. She couldn't come close to making out all the words, but it seemed to involve roses and rain. She could also hear the same gentle sound of lapping water that had accompanied their boat ride. She could smell the canal, too, damp and pleasant. For a moment she thought she was back in the boat but the seat beneath her began to steady at the same pace as her breathing did. A warm sense of well-being spread through her body as the visions began to ease up. Had she just...? Well, if she had, it was the preliminary little appetizer sort that didn't leave her properly sated.

"Any better?" Alban asked as, at last, Sylvie lifted her head.

"Yeah," Sylvie panted. "Getting there." Before she thought about what she was doing, she'd opened the top buckle of her corset to make breathing a little easier. Then she noticed Alban noticing and she met his eyes wickedly as she very slowly and deliberately opened the second buckle. "Did you still want to help?"

"Have you seen where we are?" He chuckled, though his eyes never left the gap down the front of her half-open corset.

"Is anyone likely to arrest me?" she asked, her eyes locked on his. He shook his head as he finally looked up to meet them. "Then I do...not...care." Okay, that wasn't entirely true, but...Her id savagely drowned out the dithering of the rest of her brain before it could finish that thought. "I *absolutely* do not care," she repeated, and this time she meant it without one single footnote or reservation. "All I need to know—all I *want* to know—is, are you going to help a girl out?" She bit suggestively at a fingertip while her other hand worked open the third buckle of five. "If all you wanna do is watch, though, I guess that's its own kind of fun."

Then he was kissing her hungrily, his hands fumbling at her corset while her own tore at his coat. Both items lay discarded on the floor, and she had his waistcoat half off of him before she came up for air long enough to actually glance at her surroundings. Their love seat sat in what looked like a small but nicely appointed private library lined with floor-to-ceiling bookshelves. Its chief oddity was that in addition to a few flickering gaslights the place was also lit by a row of electric footlights arrayed along what should have been the fourth wall of the library. Beyond them lay only a darkness made impenetrable by the footlights. The love seat faced the darkness head-on.

"This...is another set piece," Sylvie gasped, instinctively covering her bare chest with one arm while she tried to shade her eyes from the footlights and make out what lay beyond. "We're part of the tour?"

"Sort of," Alban panted, pushing himself up to a better sitting position. "Welcome to the front of the bleachers. This part of the canal's closed off most of the time. It only opens for the ministry's private parties. For now it's still closed. There's no one out there."

"Really? There's not?" Sylvie whimpered.

"There's not," he reassured her. He laid a hand on the arm protecting her chest, and his fingertips brushed the yielding flesh behind. Whether that part was intentional or incidental she couldn't tell—but either way, it sent a shiver through her body.

Sylvie bit at her lip again, meeting Alban's gaze wide-eyed. "Can we pretend?"

CHAPTER SIX
IT'S A DATE

"Gah! No no no no no no." Sylvie rolled over on the hotel bed and muffled a scream of frustration by burying her face in the pillow.

"What?" Nami asked, concerned by the display. They'd camped out together on a bed in Diana's suite, with Nami curled up limberly at a corner of the foot as she sorted through costuming photos on her phone, trying to decide which ones to post to her social media accounts.

"The interwebs say he's got a happily ever after," Sylvie sighed, rolling back away from the pillow and resting her own phone on her chest.

"All the good ones do." Nami offered a sympathetic smile before turning her attention back to the phone. "You just have to read a few books to know that. Anyway, Felicity says cross-world relationships make long-distance relationships look easy. I guess no one's given you that talk yet?"

"No," Sylvie pouted.

"Sorry. I got it before I went on my first world-walk. Yours must have got lost in all the crazy." Nami selected a photo, uploaded it with a quick caption, and set her phone aside. "The sex was that good, huh?"

"I didn't sa..." Sylvie started on a denial, then blushed under Nami's pointed stare. "Yes."

"So spill." Nami grinned. "You know you want to, and you know I want details."

"Have you read any of the Teprigoth books?" Sylvie asked. Nami shook her head. "It's one of those ensemble series where they change the point-of-view character a lot from book to book. Not the ongoing adventures of a single hero, but he's one of the main characters."

"Thought he was acting like it." Nami nodded. "You're stalling on the sexy bits. Share."

"He's apparently got the tragic back story. Love lost. Ladies' man who's afraid of settling down and losing it again. Classic romance-novel drama. He's got a three-book story arc where he gradually falls for Ettie Vyner, one of his co-conspirators. I even met the woman. She was sweet. I can't sabotage that." Sylvie paused wistfully for a moment, staring at the ceiling. "I think we're between the first and second book."

"Sexy bits," Nami repeated. "Share. Best girlfriends do that for each other."

"Do they?" Sylvie asked, rolling up onto one arm. "I've always felt like I've never got the whole 'best girlfriends' thing right. I had like one sleepover as a kid. Anyway, you've never told me that stuff about your dates."

"Did you ever ask?" Nami countered.

Sylvie shook her head. "I figured your sex life was none of my business."

"Well, it is now," Nami said firmly. "You know first-hand just how powerful this 'electricity' thing is now. Do you honestly think we can go poking into these worlds together and not get all up in each other's sex lives?"

"Probably not," Sylvie admitted.

"I'll be just as candid with you as you are with me. And no judging," Nami said. "Wait. Constructive judging only. We all like different stuff, but I will call you out for destructive behavior. And some stuff is just gross and weird. Have you, like, seen the internet? I don't want to hear the gross and weird stuff."

"How do I know what you think is gross and weird if we all like different stuff?" Sylvie asked.

"I'm a bisexual stripper who loves her job," Nami answered brightly. "I'm pretty broad-minded."

"You're bi too?" Sylvie asked, adding hastily, "Like Diana, I mean?"

"It was an important 'in' with the leader of the coven," Nami grinned. "I think it's also sort of a professional hazard. Too many of my customers are walking arguments for quitting men cold turkey. So, are you bi?"

Sylvie thought for a moment before deciding candor remained the best policy. "Until this weekend I'd never even asked myself that question. Pretty addicted to men, so there's half your answer. I'll have to get back to you on the rest."

"That's fair," Nami said. "Anyway, I don't want to go into a list of the stuff that grosses me out because, you know, it grosses me out. I don't mean for you to get all anatomical anyway. Speaking as a professional, I promise the brain will always be the primary erogenous zone."

"Well, if it's not a blow-by-blow you're asking for," Sylvie said.

"Nope," Nami said. "Boring."

Secure in the knowledge that the woman who'd been dropping leaden hints that they should work together in burlesque wouldn't condemn her epiphany that she was an exhibitionist, Sylvie gave in and recounted her adventures with

Alban in a fair amount of detail. By the time she got to the bit about the placement of the love seat, Nami was hanging on every word. "So I read somewhere that the average guy takes like two minutes," Sylvie said, intent now on skipping ahead past the anatomical stuff. "My actual experience has been better. Not profoundly, but better. No, I don't time them, but I think it's mostly been like five to ten."

"I'm going to guess a romance hero kind of blows that curve?" Nami prompted with a lascivious grin.

"More than a little. A lot more than a little. My knees were ready to give out before he was," Sylvie said.

"Mmm...So not missionary," Nami purred.

"We mixed it up." Sylvie found herself blushing for the umpteenth time and wondering if this level of sharing was really a good idea—also for the umpteenth time. Still, she couldn't deny it was fun reliving the experience.

"And he did get you off?" she demanded.

"Many times. Turns out he knows exactly where all the fun nerves are. The interwebs say he's some sort of psychic empath. Fictional lovers rock."

"Truth," Nami laughed. Then she caught Sylvie's questioning eye and offered, "I've had exactly one so far too. Yours sounds even better, but yeah, they seem to be hard acts to follow. Anyway, what happened after?"

"We drifted off for a bit, cuddled up on the love seat. Then we got dressed and he walked me home."

"What?!" Nami gaped. "After all that you didn't even walk around the park showing off your legs?"

"Isn't the build-up really the main event?" Sylvie asked.

Nami left her mouth hanging open for a couple of beats before snapping it closed. "Of course it is," she sighed. "Schooled by the amateur."

"I think I want to go back next week if I can and be more daring," Sylvie said. "You want to come watch? Someone mentioned you like girls."

Nami laughed. "Yes! Absolutely yes! I'll get you on the stage with me yet."

"You might," Sylvie admitted. "Maybe. I know all those feelings I was having were just me with the volume cranked all the way up, but I don't know that means I'll be getting more indulgent of that side of me out here. I still have a hard time thinking about my parents finding out. Or about lying to keep them from finding out if it came to that."

"Since you've already invited me to watch you strip off, is it okay to admit you show up in my fantasies?" Nami asked. "'Cause if it's not, I need to lock that down right now or things are going to go off the rails."

"I...I think I'm okay with that," Sylvie said with an encouraging little smile. "Not saying let's go to bed or anything, but yeah. Keep doing whatever you're doing."

"Cool. Then consider me your eager audience any time you want to let the inner exhibitionist out to play," Nami said brightly. "Moving on, let's have that facts-of-life talk. Crossing between worlds isn't easy. You've got to have the ritual and understand the ritual, and then you've got to have at least five sets of hands available for performing it. Powering the bridge eats up some stuff Diana says is expensive enough to give people pause if they're not pulling in seven figures a year. I think maybe it involves gemstones, and they shatter or something. No one's actually said. I haven't asked.

"Once you've got the bridge open, you can't count on how long it'll last. Expect a few weeks. Between Diana's investments and Felicity's star power, they do open bridges regularly; but there's no 'unlimited data plan' to fall back on. It's all pay-as-you-go. World hopping is strictly a rich-girl's game, and we're just lucky we got on the team."

"So...once this bridge closes I'm probably never setting foot in Teprigoth again, given all of the original team's bad memories of the place," Sylvie said. "Is that where this is going?"

"There and beyond," Nami said. "It gets worse. One of the team's first discoveries was, 'Take nothing. Leave nothing.' I mean, yeah, stuff can pass through, but it doesn't survive long. The souvenirs they brought home from their first trips all quietly evaporated within a couple of weeks. And taking in trade goods from our world to one of these is like dealing in faerie gold because it turns out that stuff evaporates too. We've got some rituals for extending the lifespan of stuff from other worlds but—again, those are expensive, and they're not permanent. Improving on those is apparently a big part of Diana's research. In the meantime, we work to set up on-world investments where we can. I haven't been in on that yet, but I see myself turning into a gold mine for the coven in some of these places.

"My paying skills transfer nicely between worlds, and if my clothes evaporate while I'm using them that's just a bonus." That evoked a laugh from Sylvie. "If I come home to eat, come home to sleep, then my on-world expenses add up to basically zero. Any world where I can find a club worth playing at, I can probably make enough to start a local investment portfolio while Felicity feeds my retirement fund back here in return. I don't think they've considered that arrangement yet, but it's going to be big, especially since it sounds like they've got rituals that'll keep me going past the normal expiration date for my line of work."

"A girl's gotta have a plan," Sylvie acknowledged, echoing Manami's own wisdom back to her from more than one past conversation. Nami was making really good money, but she knew she wouldn't be making really good money forever. She had hopes she'd be living off her investments by the time she was forty. That was her reason for taking a roommate when she could have made rent easily enough on her own. "My wardrobe someday going poof doesn't seem reason for that 'it gets worse', though," Sylvie said. "There's a more ominous shoe to drop?"

"Yeah," Nami said. "When the original team got mired in that whole cult thing and overstayed their bridge? They found out time takes its toll on people too. Stay too long on one of these worlds without coming back up for air and it starts gnawing at the brain. They were all mental cases before they got home: delusions, paranoias, manias, nightmarish psychedelic episodes...all sorts of bad stuff. The good news is the damage fully reversed itself within a few weeks of getting home—except apparently with Martin and maybe Sonja.

"They'd already got some hint of the mental deterioration from Loki tagging along back from his world. He had to go home for a while to let Diana work out some protection rituals. Again, not permanent and not cheap, but he'll stay sane longer than you or me. Sabbaticals at home are still part of his deal for sticking around and helping out. Oh, and Diana thinks eventually a stranded body will give out, not just the brain. No one's been willing to commit to animal testing, so that one's all a guess."

"All of which means," Sylvie said with a sigh, "even if I was ready and able to sabotage Alban's happy-ever-after, I can't stay there with him, he can't stay here with me, and sexting between rare visits won't be a coping strategy."

"Yeah. Sorry to hit you with it a bit late like this. I know it stinks, but we're never going to be more than sailors returning to port in these worlds," Nami said. "Plan your sex life accordingly."

Sylvie buried her disappointment in helping Nami sort through her costuming photos for posting. The irony of re-engaging with a fantasy convention as a way of grounding herself was not lost on her. What she really wanted to do was go out and join in a panel or something, but she'd slept through a lot of the official functions for the day and spent most of the rest of them lost in otherworldly hedonism. Entirely by luck, she'd managed to get back in time to be only a few minutes late to the costume contest she'd committed to helping with—but she'd also forgotten the cute guy who'd invited her to his game and managed to stand him up entirely.

She'd definitely need to take tomorrow to deal with the mundane world. All of which reminded her she wasn't finished dealing with the practical details of her induction into the world of the arcane. Once Nami had assembled her new little gallery of customer-bait photos, Sylvie excused herself to go looking for one of the senior partners. It didn't take long. Felicity seemed to be on a phone call in the room where they'd slept the morning away, talking loudly enough for Sylvie to guess it was probably about an acting project. Sylvie found a television remote and settled in to wait out the call.

When Felicity finally appeared, she didn't so much walk out of her room as glide out of it like some steampunk goddess, her long, golden curls framing that angelic face in a crowning halo. Her flowing Victorianish dress traded the lingerie vibe for a classical muse one, while retaining a touch of the mad scientist. This was not the steampunk costume she'd been wearing on the first night, which had been more modest than Sylvie's but still risqué by Victorian standards. This one wouldn't quite blend with the fashions Sylvie had seen at the park, but surely it would only draw admiring attention, not critical.

Seeing Sylvie there, Felicity favored her with a glowing smile. "How are you adjusting?" she asked as Sylvie flicked off the television.

"Okay, I think," Sylvie said. "We're still waiting to hear back from Loki?"

"Basically," Felicity said. "He's checked in, but we still only know places that Martin isn't. I think he's consciously avoiding our old haunts, and it's a huge city. Even with an army of cats hunting him I'm starting to worry he might have managed to slip away with the book."

"Are you free to help me get oriented then?" Sylvie asked.

"Sure." Felicity smiled again—it really was a devastating smile—and pulled up a seat on the far corner of the couch. "What can I do for you?"

"To start, I'm obliged to spend a lot of tomorrow ferrying convention guests back to the airport. The day after tomorrow, though, what then? I've got a job. I've got rent and all those other things to pay. Right now, everything's all freewheeling adventure but when I come back down where do I land? Is this coven thing a job or a hobby or a university or what? Will I need to move to be part of it? I desperately want to be in on this, but how will I afford it?"

"All good questions," Felicity said. "We're still making this up as we go, putting together the new team. I'm the money, though. Talk to me about what you need, and we'll work things out. Your time and training are valuable, but I like partners more than employees. It's a much more comfortable dynamic for me. There's tons of money to be made here, and I'm afraid that if we talk salary rather than percentage that will someday boil over into resentment.

"How's this for a start? I call up and book your limo for a month so you can forget about work for a while. After that, all of this is going to be easiest if the coven sets up in an L.A.-area headquarters. I could pull some strings and get you and Nami good work out there. Have you ever thought of being a stunt woman?"

"I...hadn't, no," Sylvie said. "Now that you mention it that sounds amazing."

"Good. Don't give your two-weeks' notice yet, but I'll make sure you're covered at work," Felicity said. "And as to this being a university, yes, it's sort of that. We're all here to learn and to experiment. There's no formal curriculum, but once we've got the Martin situation contained we'll work together to get you up to speed. Just to give you a frame of reference, there's no magic wands or spell-slinging involved like at Lovelace. Everything we've figured out is ritualized: slow and meticulous and dangerous to get even a little bit wrong. No one's been killed or maimed by it yet, but we had enough close calls early on to learn a healthy respect for the whole process. Take your time, do it right—do it exactly right—or random things will happen. When random things powered by arcane magic happen, they're almost always bad. We only make progress by changing a single small variable at a time and paying close attention to the results."

"Okay. Good. Thank you. That's all a load off," Sylvie said. "Now can I ask—"

"I just like girls," Felicity said, interrupting her. "Kassia just likes guys. Everyone knows Diana likes everyone. You probably know better than me what Nami likes. I'll know what you like when you tell me. Sorry, that's just the obvious bit that's a bit awkward. Best to get it out of the way given where all this takes us."

"I guess so." Sylvie chuckled. "It wasn't going to be my first question, but good to know. I very much like guys. I found it very cozy waking up beside you. I'll tell you anything more if and when I figure it out."

"That works," Felicity said. Her smile was its own sort of seduction. It was a career-making smile. You didn't have to want her to want to drown in it. Without saying a word, she could wrap you up in it, reassure you everything was going to turn out all right, and let you know she was the sympathetic ear that would always be on your side.

That was an illusion of course. She couldn't possibly be always on the side of everyone she'd unleashed that smile on. That didn't stop it from being practically erotic in its intimacy. Felicity had been known for her mesmerizing smile since her debut in the first Lovelace film, but if anything it had gotten even more potent since then. Was that just naturally her, or had she used magic to achieve the effect? Diana had mentioned something about beauty spells...

"Well, I guess if Kassia's straight at least I'm not the only girl here who hasn't kissed Diana Taylor." Sylvie smirked, consciously shaking off the effect of Felicity's smile.

"A vanishing breed," Felicity laughed. "Kissing Diana is not a requirement, but it's not a coincidence either. She'll mix business and pleasure in a heartbeat if you let her. She's always been like that. I find it's a dangerous mix personally, but this world-hopping bit almost demands it—what with the expense, the teamwork, and la química, as Kassia likes to call it. That name's growing on me, by the way."

"My first question was actually going to be about my friend, Brian," Sylvie said. "He got himself shot over all this and I haven't even figured out yet what to tell him. I haven't figured out yet what I can tell him. All I know is he's seen enough and he's smart enough that he's going to hit me with tons of questions as soon as I see him again. It sounds like that'll be tomorrow morning. I know I'd be on thin ice at best to just blurt out the full, unfiltered truth. As far as you're concerned, what are my options? How secret is this secret society thing?"

"We sort of count on it to be self-policing," Felicity said. "The official line is it doesn't exist. The official tantalizing tabloid secret if we need to let the conspiracy theorists uncover one is it's an illicit sex club. The official line of defense if anyone tries to claim we're a coven of magicians is to collapse in uncontrollable fits of laughter. So, no, this doesn't need to turn into any of that 'tell painful lies to your loved ones to protect your secret identity' nonsense. Your friend saw what he saw. Don't insult his intelligence. Ask him to keep the secret and make it clear that we can arrange for all sort of expert testimony to declare that any evidence he leaks is computer special effects and that any testimony he might give is the ravings of a madman. I've got a couple of discrete investors with even deeper pockets than mine, and they won't hesitate to fight dirty."

"Money touches everything, doesn't it?" Sylvie asked.

"Money touches everything," Felicity agreed.

"Am I free to take him back through the portal if he brings it up?" Sylvie asked.

"Make sure he's dressed appropriately. Borrow protection for him from Diana. Don't explain it to him, just tell him it's a non-negotiable insurance policy. We're not where we can give out magic trinkets to just anyone. And be sure before you take him that you've thought through the ramifications."

"Of...?" Sylvie prompted.

"All of it," Felicity said. "But especially la química."

"Just so we're clear, this is an actual date?" Brian asked, adjusting the waistcoat of the steampunk costume Sylvie had just bought him from the dealer room on Felicity's dime. It was the morning of the final day of the convention, and they were standing in the outer room of Diana's suite, making final adjustments to their costumes.

"Close enough," Sylvie said. She'd picked up a more modest outfit for herself while they were picking out Brian's. Like Felicity's, it wouldn't exactly blend, but it should be close enough for a casual visit. "I think I can waive the roller-coaster test for a guy who got himself shot for me. There's a lot of overlap."

Brian was doing fine. He was on some really nice pain killers, but the actual damage had been limited and the blood loss hadn't been severe. The simple shock to his system had been the worst of it. He had his arm in a sling to remind him not to use it. "Also, so we're clear, I didn't really take a bullet for you," he said. "You know that, right?"

"Splitting hairs," she assured him. "I asked you to come have my back on an adventure. You came. Doesn't matter that you didn't expect a bullet before it was too late to do anything. For all you knew, we were going to get ambushed by some supernatural psychopath with machetes for hands when we walked in there. It would have fit the narrative. Adventure means risk. You took it. That's better than climbing on the wildest roller coaster in the state with me. If I wasn't planning to move to L.A. I'd be willing to rethink our whole lack of relationship. But knowing what I know about this place now, I can't take you in there and insist it's not a date. If you can live with knowing this is strictly a short-term thing, a date is what it is. If you can't, we'd better rethink the whole expedition."

"What if I wind up in L.A. myself?" he asked.

"I won't promise anything, and I won't owe you anything if you do, so don't do it for me," she said sternly. "But if you happen to show up in a couple of years and we're both still single, I have no plans at this moment to close that door. Fair enough?"

"Yeah," he said. "It'll do. So what do you know about it that makes this a date?"

"Remember the Interstellar 2000 episode where everyone's inhibitions drop to zero?" she asked.

"Of course," he said.

"That."

A few minutes later and a few explanations more found them stepping out onto the misty Sunday morning streets of Teprigoth. A few passersby passed by, more or less minding their own business, while Brian gawked at everything like the tourist he was.

"Yes," Sylvie assured him. "Magic is absolutely real."

"Now you know I'm coming to L.A. when I can," he said. "You don't have to date me, but you can't show me this then shut me out."

"I suppose not," Sylvie admitted, giving herself a good mental thump to the head for not having immediately reached that conclusion on her own. She'd never have let Diana just walk away after seeing this herself. "This isn't my magic though. Not yet. And I'll never be able to take you world hopping without the blessing of the others. I promise we'll stay in touch and talk about this more, but that's all I can promise right now, okay?"

Brian nodded, mollified.

"Diana says that if the cats don't find Martin before then she'll break out the heavier rituals this afternoon to track him down." Sylvie had brought Brian more or less up to speed on the overall Martin problem. "With her commitment to the con done, she'll be able to focus."

"So what's the etiquette here?" Brian asked. "Can a gentleman offer a lady an arm?"

Brian accepted her taking his already-proffered good arm as an answer. There was no pity factor involved in Sylvie calling this a date. Now clean shaven, Brian had gone from 'cute enough' to fairly dashing in his Victorianish outfit. She'd never stopped liking him, either, and she could already feel la química hard at work leveraging those two simple facts into something more...complicated...so she clung contentedly to his arm as they strolled down the street, and she allowed herself to be happy. No one could mistake Brian for a romance-novel hero. That was okay. He was inarguably real. She could ground herself with him in a way she really needed right now.

Plus, if things did get out of hand with him before she moved to L.A. there'd be nothing stopping her from sexting him.

"What's that grin about?" Brian asked.

"Nothing," Sylvie said, perhaps a bit too quickly. "I'm just with a good friend sharing an adventure that we'd have thought was completely out of reach when we showed up at the hotel on Friday. Oh, and, you know—Interstellar 2000."

"Miss Grove, are you having inappropriate thoughts already?" he asked in a feeble attempt at feigning Victorian moral indignation.

"Just little ones," she giggled.

"I never actually stopped having inappropriate thoughts about you, so I'm not sure I'll know when this place tries to give me those," Brian said.

"We'll figure something out." Sylvie laughed, patting him reassuringly on the shoulder. The looks they were getting told her she was pushing it with the displays of affection, but she found she didn't much care. It wasn't like she had to live here. "So what do you want to see? I've got maybe three hours before I have to be back playing chauffeur. There's a really cool amusement park, but we've got like zero money to actually ride anything. There's a cathedral over there." She pointed out its silhouette towering above the local buildings, hazily visible through the mist. "I'm told there's a whole entertainment district on beyond the park, but I'm not sure how far or how easy it would be to find. Or we can just wander around and explore if we're careful not to get lost."

"If you've already seen the amusement park, let's check out the cathedral," Brian said. "That'll make it something new for both of us, and maybe we can figure out money for the amusement park on another day."

In lieu of leaving a trail of lipstick marks this time, Sylvie had come prepared with a small notepad in which she kept a crude diagram of the streets to help them retrace their steps. Soon they'd left the wealthy residences behind them and had merged with a heavier mix of middle-class foot traffic, horse-drawn carts and carriages, and the occasional trolley laden with an abundance of unidentifiable mechanical embellishments in addition to its human cargo. Once in a while a robotic worker would clank by, intent on its menial task. If Sylvie and Brian drew overmuch attention at any point, they never had to endure it long before the mist swallowed up any given audience to be replaced by a whole new set of strangers. A gentle rain added itself to the misty atmosphere, neither cold enough nor strong enough to send them running for cover.

"This is great," Brian said, smiling at her. "Seeing all this and picking up where we left off. You feel good on my arm."

"It is nice," Sylvie agreed, returning the smile.

"Can I ask what the big deal with the 'roller coaster' test even is?" Brian said. "It's that important to you that a guy's willing to ride through seven corkscrews and plummet straight down a hundred feet?"

Sylvie chewed at her lip for a bit. "I guess it's my dad," she said finally.

"Your dad doesn't like roller coasters?" Brian asked.

"Loves them," Sylvie said. "I get the whole adrenaline-junkie thing from him. It's my mom that hates roller coasters. Mom loves fantasy stories and all this convention stuff. Dad doesn't get them. I guess it's kind of cool that I have this thing where I get Dad all to myself for a while and I have this thing where I get Mom all to myself for a while, but it hurts sometimes too because we don't have anything like that for the whole family to get passionate about. And they've got a good marriage and all, but...they can be distant sometimes, too. I just can't help wondering how epic it would be if they really got into each other's passions. I don't want to wake up one day and find I've committed to living parallel lives with somebody. I just don't. We're friends because we've got the fantasy stuff in common, but I need my roller coasters."

"There was a time I'd have tried the big ones with you," Brian said. "They were always intimidating, but...you know those 'squirrel cages'? Like a Ferris wheel but the seats are enclosed?"

"That spin completely upside down and around and reverse directions? Love 'em," Sylvie said.

"Those. I tried one once," Brian said. "It was fun, but when I stepped off I thought I was going to throw up. I never did, but I wished I had because that's exactly how I felt for the rest of the day. I was completely miserable until I'd slept it off. I've gotten motion sick pretty easily ever since. If the roller coaster test was like a courage challenge, okay. I'd be miserable for a day for you. I can't make a life of that, though."

"Oh," Sylvie said pensively. "Sorry."

"Me too," he said. "So how many guys do you think are going to pass the world-hopping test?"

Sylvie bit back a caustic reply just before it could come bursting out of her mouth, and she remained silent instead. The remark had hurt. Worse, there'd been just enough edge in his voice to betray that he'd wanted it to. But maybe she'd earned it. She couldn't deny the truth that her vision of a perfect romance had just become absurdly more complicated by all of this.

"Can we agree right now that we're not going to push the relationship—or non-relationship or whatever this is—any further while we're here, though?" Brian asked, moving the conversation on before Sylvie could sink too far into dark introspection. He seemed aware that his tone had a gone a bit rogue on what had probably sounded like a simple, straightforward question in his brain. "No new milestones? No lines crossed? I've been thinking about what you've said about this place. I don't want to get home and find I'm trying to sort out what meant something from what might not have."

"A very good point." Sylvie nodded, rallying her emotions. She also refrained from asking how many lines they could even cross in the next two hours because, well, Alban. "Agreed. Yes." She'd already let her feelings about Alban get more complicated than she was entirely comfortable with, and those were destined to become irrelevant soon enough. Letting this place distort her relationship with a man she couldn't reasonably cut out of her life any time soon did sound like a profoundly bad idea.

Sylvie became aware that at some point they'd merged into a steadily growing stream of people headed in the direction of the cathedral, and it dawned on her that if the local religion and calendar were analogous, the crowds would be on their way to some Sunday morning service. It became more evident still when they emerged into the grand plaza in front of the cathedral to find crowds converging from all sides and making their way up the steps to the great doors of the cathedral. Sylvie and Brian quickly agreed it might be best to remain playing tourist from the outside rather than intrude on that, and they broke from the flow of foot traffic to wander about the edges of the building as the bells began to toll overhead.

The general size and shape of the details visible through the fog largely fit Sylvie's expectations of a Gothic cathedral, down to the numerous gargoyle rain spouts. Enough rain had fallen by this point that it emerged from their mouths in a steady trickle to spatter on the cobbles below. The sculptures she'd expected to resolve out of the haze into the form of saints as she drew closer, though, turned out to look more like river nymphs and mermaids amid a scattering of less name-able aquatic creatures that back home would most certainly be things of myth. Here, it would be premature for her to guess whether any of them were fanciful or factual.

"It's quite something, isn't it?" a woman standing beside them asked as she peered out from under her umbrella at the architecture. "Sylvie, wasn't it?"

Sylvie did a double-take and realized she was standing beside Ettie Vyner. The woman had traded her bright blue dress of the day before for an even brighter blue, bordering on electric. "Yes," she agreed before anticipating Ettie's next query and introducing her to Brian.

"Are you on your way to services?" Ettie asked. Sylvie shook her head. "Me either. It's a beautiful building but not always welcoming. I've just got business at the library."

"There's a library?" Brian asked, his interest instantly perked.

"An archive, I suppose," Ettie said. "The cathedral keeps most of the public records for the ward in its vaults. No place to go looking for penny dreadfuls but it's a treasure trove for scholars."

"So there's a big library?" Brian grinned.

Ettie laughed. "There's a big library. I haven't come close to seeing it all."

Sylvie checked her pocket watch. “We’ve got maybe an hour to kill. Would they let us look around?”

“Sure,” Ettie said. “It’s pretty much a public resource even if most of the public has no interest in it.” She led the way around toward the back of the cathedral and in through a street-level door. It opened into a small vestibule that then opened into the second story of a breathtaking, two-story vaulted gallery that ran the entire width of the cathedral. A spiral staircase led down from the balcony level to the cellar level, both of which were lined with shelf after shelf after shelf of books. It seemed no expense had been spared in illuminating the place with electric light fixtures to protect its contents from any chance encounter with an open flame. The gallery smelled distinctly of vanilla.

They’d gone a few paces in, their voices echoing off the vaulted ceiling though they reflexively spoke among themselves in hushed tones, when a woman appeared from out of the stacks and held a finger to her lips. “Hush,” she admonished gently. “The books are trying to sleep.” Something about the auburn-haired woman and her large, round spectacles immediately put Sylvie in mind of a big-eyed anime character.

“Hi, Wambleesha,” Ettie greeted her in the same subdued tone she’d already been using. “This is Sylvie. That’s Brian. They’ll try not to wake the books.”

“Oh!” Wambleesha brightened as she seemed to take notice of the two of them for the first time. “Are you here to see the man in the cellars or the woman in the belfry?”

“I, uh...Yes?” Sylvie stammered quietly.

“They’re just here to see the archive,” Ettie assured the woman before adding even more quietly as an aside to Sylvie, “She’s a great archivist, but she doesn’t get out much.” Ettie punctuated the last with a discrete hand gesture to intimate that was a polite way of putting it.

"Actually, I'm curious about both those people," Sylvie said quickly. One of the strictest rules of narrative was to never dismiss the ramblings of the apparently insane. Sometimes they only seemed insane, and always they knew something important that you didn't. If the bridge had specifically gone looking for Alban to fit an archetypal character in a book, it struck Sylvie as far-fetched to believe she hadn't just been introduced to another archetype in Wambleesha. Regardless of whether the archivist had been born into a narrative or the narrative had come seeking her out, it should all be one and the same.

"Hey, if that's your thing," Ettie said with a quiet little chuckle. "I've got some research to do."

Sylvie found Brian glancing back and forth between her and Ettie as the other woman turned to go. "Go," she told him. "See your books. Just meet me back here in an hour. Remember, I've got the map." She shooed him off after Ettie. He responded with a smile and a nod before heading out.

"So...Wambleesha? Did I pronounce that right?" Sylvie asked. "I don't think I've met anyone named Wambleesha before." She was very sure she hadn't. "So what was this about a man and a woman?"

Wambleesha seemed slightly nonplussed that Ettie had bailed and left her talking to a stranger. Sylvie took notice and tried to dial back the friendly. While Wambleesha was still working to sort out the rush of questions, Sylvie stepped aside to pull up a chair at a handy reading table, hoping that a lower elevation and more relaxed posture would make her seem less intimidating. Fandom had long been used as a safe haven by introverts, and Sylvie had befriended her share. You basically had to treat them like cats. "I honestly don't know who you're talking about," Sylvie continued patiently, "but I bet you know a lot of important things that most people don't take as seriously as they should. So will you tell me about them?"

"Really?" The surprise was so evident on Wambleesha's face that Sylvie half expected her to physically transform from generic anime character into an over-excited child-like chibi. It didn't happen.

"Yes. Absolutely." Sylvie gestured to the chair across the table from her. Worst case scenario for Sylvie, she'd lose an hour she would have spent admiring shelves full of tax records and a bit of architecture. "You said one of them was upstairs and one of them was downstairs?"

"Yes," Wambleesha agreed, hesitantly taking the chair but seeming to warm a bit at being called on as a subject matter expert. "They're both strange like you."

"You mean the clothes?" Sylvie asked, remembering that she still didn't really blend.

Wambleesha gave a little shrug and adjusted her spectacles. "Is that how you're strange?"

Right. The archivist wouldn't exactly have blended with the crowd on the street either. Her eclectic outfit was a little bit Goth, a little bit Victorian, a little bit crazed candy entrepreneur, and one-hundred percent 'I got dressed in the dark'. "Bad question," Sylvie admitted. "What makes me seem strange to you?"

"You smell...not bad, but wrong. Out of place. Different," Wambleesha said. "Like you're dragging a thunderstorm behind you. That's how they smell too. And the woman kind of smells like snow."

Delusion, some sort of psychic sense, or just the sensory displacement of synesthesia, Sylvie wondered? She fancied the synesthesia explanation but would try to stay open to the other possibilities. "Do you actually know them?" she asked. "Do you talk to them? Or have you just seen them?"

"I haven't seen the man in a long time. Never really talked to him. I still hear him sometimes deep down in the archives. He talks to the books. I'm not sure he listens."

Okay, she's doubled down on anthropomorphizing the books, Sylvie noted. Again, that could be anything from quirky delusion to indulging a role-play of what passed for her stuffed animal collection to something mystical, either miraculous or sinister. Sylvie remained confident the woman knew important things, but teasing out those truths from the colorful personality promised to be quite a challenge. "And the woman?" she prompted.

"She's nice," the archivist said. "We've talked a few times. Sometimes she has visitors who smell like her. They fly up to visit her in the tallest spire. Just by night though, or people would make a fuss."

"Do any of these people have names?" Sylvie asked.

"Yes," Wambleesha answered. "Most people do. I would imagine they need them."

"Do you know any of those names?" Sylvie urged.

"Just the woman in the tower," Wambleesha said. Sylvie held her gaze until she got the hint and volunteered more. "Lark," Wambleesha said. "She calls herself Lark."

Precisely thirty-nine seconds later Sylvie had caught up to Brian and was shoving her map into his hands. "Go. Go! Get Diana. Get Felicity, Get everybody! I'll meet you back here."

"Why? What's going on?" Brian demanded.

"I don't have any idea at all," Sylvie said, "but I'm going to find out. Coincidences don't happen to us here."

CHAPTER SEVEN
TOWER OF DREAMS

Sylvie had tried doing it the easy way. She really had—but the tower door had been locked. What sort of rogue was she for the party if she couldn't pick a simple, utilitarian old lock? That was one skill she was going to have to teach herself in short order because sometimes a girl actually *wanted* to do things the easy way. Right now Sylvie could have been making her way leisurely up a long, winding staircase, but...Stop. If she was going to be perfectly honest with herself this was fun. It was insane, but it was fun. She should probably seek a professional opinion about her self-destructive behavior when she got home. If she got home.

The foolishness had started before she'd even begun climbing because there was absolutely no way to do this in a sensible Victorian dress; so that now lay neatly folded beneath a chair in the archive's vestibule. She'd stripped as soon as she'd had the little room to herself, and now she was scaling the back of a Gothic cathedral in what might as well have been Victorian London wearing the same sports bra and bike shorts she might have gone jogging in back in Vegas. The only mercy of having worn that dress was it had been long enough she'd dared wear really good shoes under it—so she was even wearing her workout shoes for the climb. Had her ascent been concealed by cover of night then she probably wouldn't have had enough light to risk it, so climbing in this gray fog was probably the best she could have hoped for though she had no guarantee it mightn't finally decide to lift at any moment, leaving her exposed halfway up the wall. Sylvie shivered, her stomach lurching like she'd just crested a hill on a roller coaster as the thought triggered seldom dredged up memories of April Shand.

A schoolmate several years Sylvie's senior who had long since disappeared from her life, April had been the primary object of Sylvie's hero worship before she'd decided she wanted to grow up to be Lark Starling. Sylvie had never known much about the girl's family or personal life, had been too far behind her to even know which cliques she'd moved in at school, but when Sylvie had been a pre-teen April had definitely been the coolest teenager willing to give her the time of day.

One of the most awesome things April had been into was rock-wall climbing, and one of the moments etched forever into Sylvie's memory was April tousling her hair encouragingly after Sylvie's rather pathetic attempt to scale the climbing wall set up at the spring festival. That was the moment just before April had stood up to show off her own skills on the wall, leaving an empty space on the bench next to her boyfriend, Tim, who Sylvie had been quietly crushing on for the last month. Sylvie had wasted no time in claiming the seat for herself, and then studiously tried to avoid getting caught looking at him. On the other side of Tim sat one of his buddies whose name Sylvie had never caught, and while they all watched April climb Sylvie could hear him ribbing Tim with some envious and crude remarks about the view of his girlfriend. The remarks had made Sylvie uncomfortable, but to Tim's credit he tried gently but repeatedly to shut the boy down. At the time it had seemed practically chivalrous. Finally, with April halfway up the wall, the boy said, "Her family's nudists, you know."

"Shut up," Tim had warned him, the long-suffering tone in his previous warnings taking on an edge.

"Serious," the boy had insisted. "She runs around naked all summer at that place down by the lake. Wanna bet she goes climbing like that too?"

"Serious," Tim had echoed. "I'm about to deck you. No kidding." The boy finally went silent, but the next time Sylvie avoided getting caught looking at Tim it was pretty obvious that his mind had checked out. There could be no mistaking where it had gone or how thoroughly Tim had undressed April with his eyes as she finished her climb. Sylvie never found out or cared if there'd been an ounce of truth in the boy's claims. The truth of them didn't matter. What mattered was that look on Tim's face and how much Sylvie wished she'd been April up there on the receiving end.

Coming back to the present, Sylvie waffled through an internal monologue with herself on whether it was really fair to call this architectural style Gothic. Eventually, she decided it didn't matter. It was Gothic-ish in the same way her steampunk costume was Victorianish. The relevant part was that it was ornate, liberally employing buttresses and flying buttresses, statuary, arches, and alcoves. Everywhere she turned there were handholds and chimneys just begging to be climbed. If she'd had a safety line, this whole building would have been one big playground.

She didn't have a safety line, though, and the rain had left everything damp and the security of her grip and footing in doubt. That made the climb deadly serious business. She had to make doubly sure of every step and every handhold before she trusted it. The probability of a mishap didn't trouble her. The same could not be said for the consequences if a mishap *did* occur. Somehow, though, that queasy feeling in her gut just egged her on. She couldn't turn away from the climb any more than she could have held back with Alban if she'd found out they'd had an audience beyond those footlights.

It was with some small disappointment that Sylvie made it up to the first section of slate roof without any sign she'd attracted attention. Anyone on the street who saw her now, from this distance in this fog, would probably just take her for a gargoyle come to life to flit across the rooftop. Much further up and no one below would be able to see her at all.

The tiles here seemed solid enough, and she crossed them cautiously without any loss of footing. The next climb offered very little chance of exposure in the fog. It wasn't as long as the first climb either, but the wall was less ornate so it offered fewer handholds. If she fell, she'd probably survive hitting the roof. Then she'd probably roll headlong off the edge and not survive hitting the cobbles. She spent some time looking around for a way in from this level but found none. In the end, she decided on shimmying up a decorative chimney in a buttress.

She'd gotten about halfway and was catching her breath, wedged in with her feet pressed against one side of the chimney and her back against the other, when a large black bird decided she looked like a more attractive perch than the usual gargoyles. Without fear and without introduction or other niceties, it simply dropped down as if to land talons-out on her exposed stomach. Instinctively Sylvie swatted it away, and for one heart-stopping moment felt her whole body shift along with her shoulder. The bird took the hint, though, and she re-anchored herself by pressing harder with her legs before she even knew she was doing it. She made it to the second section of roof and allowed herself to just sprawl back on it while she recovered physically and mentally, staring up at the bell tower and the endless gray haze that surrounded it. Even from here she couldn't make out the top in any detail. It remained just a silhouette in the fog.

If she couldn't find a way inward from here, would she press on? Going back was still an option and still safer than continuing up. There was also no way of knowing if the climb would become impossible before she reached the opening for the bells. She knew the answer before she even asked herself the question though. This was her job. This was why she was on the team. More than that, every fiber of her being was singing at the sheer audacity of the adventure. Sylvie Grove had not spent her life waiting for magic to happen just to sit around waiting again to see if that magic included an incantation to get through a locked door. This was her mountain to conquer. She was climbing it because it was there.

More even than all that, the universe had abruptly offered up the hope of realizing her schoolgirl dream of meeting the actual, original, real Lark Starling in the flesh just when the relentless weight of the adult world had been forcing her to come to grips with the truth it could never happen. If she waited for back-up, any hope of Sylvie meeting Lark would be out the window. It would be Sylvie's team meeting Lark. That wouldn't be the same at all.

As she crawled back to her feet and began to carefully assess the climb ahead of her, she found herself gripped with doubt about this being Lark Starling, where she'd so recently felt certain it could be no other Lark—but even if the rules of the narrative didn't apply to this situation, she wanted to find that out right here and right now. Physically she could retreat. Emotionally she was completely boxed in. There could be no way for her now but up.

The good news was that the ornate decoration that had been missing on the last stretch of Sylvie's climb resumed in full force on the tower. Without a backward glance, and before she could second-guess herself, she began the final ascent. Foot by hard-won foot the tower yielded to her determination until hardly anything remained in her universe but that one sheer wall stretching up and down into gray oblivion.

Alone with the gargoyles and the water nymphs, Sylvie paused and rested at each ledge, nursing her strength for both the climb ahead and what might be an unavoidable return trip. The fog must have played havoc on her initial guess of the tower's height because she still found herself climbing long after she'd been sure she should have reached the belfry. Once or twice the shadow of a large bird glided past in the fog. Several times some statue—glimpsed out of the corner of Sylvie's eye—seemed to shift, only to regard her with stony stillness when she turned to focus on it. She quickly despaired of sorting out whether it was the isolation playing tricks on her mind, whether such things were simply a fact of life in this world, or whether her mind was already showing the first hint of deterioration at being away from home.

The higher she climbed the more disconcerting it all became, but it became more exhilarating just as quickly. Increasingly she found she was under a spell like a runner's high, pushing herself through that tense and punishing marathon that no one in her right mind would have even set out on, chasing the ecstasy of accomplishment.

Above her, the bells in the belfry tolled, thunderously near, and Sylvie desperately linked elbows with a mermaid so that she could cover her ears. Given that the tolling of the bells marked the passage of time it dawned on her that she'd already been at this too long. She'd never make it back in time to finish out her commitment as the convention's chauffeur. Well, they could bill her for the rides. She couldn't be sorry.

When the tolling of the bells had passed, and with the hope that her goal was just out of sight, Sylvie turned her attention back to the wall and began planning her next grip. Behind her someone giggled. Slowly, carefully, she craned to look over first one shoulder, then the other. All remained gray, empty mist.

Was it her imagination, or could she hear faint whispers drifting out of it? Diana's words, "Dangerous in its subtlety," wandered through her mind. There might be absolutely nothing out there right now, but Sylvie had worked very hard to put herself in a place where something as simple as her own imagination could kill her. Another knot tied itself in her stomach, but she could hardly make herself more vulnerable if she tried. The worst move she could make right now would be to freeze in fear. She forced herself to ignore the emptiness behind her and returned to clawing her way up the wall.

More giggling. More whispering. If it was her imagination it was no longer playing coy about it. She'd slipped on over into delusion. Then at last, the broad arch of the belfry appeared out of the mist. She paused. She breathed. She thought.

"All right," she said quietly to herself. "This is the part where..." Yes, there was one final gargoyle to haul herself up by, and she'd be able to reach the railing. She stopped her ascent. If she was going to die here it would be by her own idiocy, not in the service of some ironic narrative. Avoiding the obvious path, she began to edge along a tiny ledge, picking every handhold with care and patience. Only when she reached the next strategically placed gargoyle over did she continue upward. Seconds later, she was pulling herself over the archway's low railing and into the belfry, where she collapsed with her heart pounding in her chest, listening to the faint whispers that still followed her out of the fog.

She'd probably never know if there'd been anything gained by skirting that final gargoyle. That was okay. She'd also never know what her life would be like if she'd walked away from Diana's invitation. Some things just weren't worth the risk. That last thought set her into painful convulsions of laughter at its juxtaposition with the sheer hubris that had driven her up here. Unable to shut down the spasms of nervous laughter,

Sylvie curled up into a ball trying to minimize the pain, and she rode them out.

When at last the spasms stopped and her breathing had begun to steady, she slowly uncurled and rolled once more onto her back. She opened her eyes to find herself staring into the face of a ghost. She gasped but felt no urge to scream. It was a face from a thousand teenage fantasies that her adult dreams had never entirely abandoned. It was the face of the man supposedly buried in Avalon, who had lent its dark hair, piercing eyes, and bronze complexion to Lark Starling's Isaac Rush for half a dozen movies. It hovered not six inches above her own face, and Sylvie could feel the warm flesh of its associated fingers as they gently closed her gaping mouth. "I love your laugh," he said with a smile, his eyes meeting hers unflinchingly.

Sylvie tried to form words in response, but they never coalesced in her mind, much less reached her lips. Instead she found herself kissing him passionately, unaware and unconcerned for which of them had started it. It was a dream. It had always been a dream. This was the dream she'd had countless times before where she *was* Lark Starling, tearing at Isaac's clothes while he tore at hers in the wake of their first successful Robin-Hood-esque heist. On screen it had been on the roof of a skyscraper, but her dreams never hesitated to shake up the specifics of the setting. The only real criteria was it had to be dizzyingly high. Those first frantic moments of passion were all that had appeared on screen before the fade to black, but that had only left more permutations for Sylvie's fantasies to explore.

This time those fantasies just happened to bring her to a cathedral spire and just happened to achieve whole new levels of sensory clarity. She could actually smell the damp stones of the cathedral, feel the cool, wooden scaffolding beneath her, hear her own breath rasping excitedly past her teeth as she helped him wrestle her out of the sports bra. She could feel the annoyingly secure binding of her shoelaces as she struggled to kick them off without letting Isaac out of her embrace. When she succeeded, she could hear one of them bounce carelessly away down the central shaft of the bell tower.

There was no pretense of courtship here. They'd already been there. This was the moment of mutual surrender when they moved past all that. It was raw. It was urgent. It was forceful. It was beyond intense. Everything it lacked in duration and art on the Alban fantasy it more than made up for as the fulfillment of a pent-up yearning that had been kept in check for the better part of a decade, for no other reason than it seemed utterly impossible to fulfill.

When the last echoes of her own impassioned screams had finally died away, when she had felt Isaac roll away as she lay with her eyes closed, panting for breath, she heard a creak of wooden stairs as someone unhurriedly ascended them, and she wondered if she should care.

"Hey, Holly," she heard her own voice say. "All good up there? I was about to head for bed when I, umm...heard you guys. You know the sound-proofing's good, but it's not *that* good." She heard herself laugh. Only then did she start to remember she wasn't really Lark Starling, and that the voice wasn't hers to lay claim to.

Suddenly Sylvie found herself sitting bolt upright, alone on the wooden walkway of the cathedral belfry, naked save for a single sock she hadn't kicked off. She couldn't account for Isaac's whereabouts, though the walkway would have told her both by sound and vibration if he'd gotten up or rolled further away. One of the shoes she'd kicked off hung precariously on the edge of the walkway, and she retained enough memory to know what had happened to the other. The other sock and her workout wear that had been slung so carelessly aside could as easily have followed her shoe down the shaft or gone flying out of the tower altogether.

"Holly?" the voice called again from directly below her. It sounded just like Diana but without any of the British accent. It was the actual Lark Starling, the woman she'd come here to see. And not only was Sylvie naked; she was naked because she'd just fallen into raw animal sex with Lark's boyfriend—or at least thought she had. In her defense, Sylvie had let herself get so swept up in the moment that she had really, truly forgotten he wasn't her own boyfriend. And now she couldn't even prove he had been there at all. Even the clothes she'd torn him out of had disappeared more completely than hers had. At one and the same time, she both had to and didn't dare make contact with the woman she'd come to see, so like any sensible person she froze, her brain locked into indecision until reality took the choice out of her hands.

"Okay," Lark said as she finished mounting the stairs. "I'm pretty sure you're not Holly." Her signature unruly curls were working overtime on the unruly part, and a lavender dressing gown flowed down the full length of her body.

"I, uh...No," Sylvie stammered, realizing she'd curled up to hide behind her own legs.

"Huh." Lark's shrug showed on her face more than it did in her shoulders. "You're one I haven't seen before. Keep it down, will you? I don't need sleep deprivation on top of everything else." Message delivered, she turned and headed back down the stairs.

"Wait!" Sylvie called out, crawling to peek out over the edge of the walkway. Lark turned to peer back up at her expectantly. Again, Sylvie's head failed to form any sort of useful, coherent thought. Lark shrugged again, this time with her shoulders fully engaged, and headed on down the stairs. Well, Sylvie had wanted people to look at her, and Lark had seemed entirely unfazed by finding a naked woman on her roof. Sylvie rescued her remaining shoe from the brink, pulled off the ludicrous lone sock and stuffed it into the shoe, then got up and hurried down the stair after Lark. A couple of turns down, Lark stepped off into an alcove by a landing. By the time Sylvie arrived, Lark had stepped through a door there. Sylvie followed her into a fire-lit sitting room, narrow but cozy, that seemed to extend back under the stairs.

Spying Sylvie, Lark let out a little sigh. "I don't sleep with women. You know that, right?"

"Does that, umm, mean you do sleep with more than one man?" Sylvie asked. "Because I thought Isaac..."

"Isaac is Isaac. Men are men. Sometimes a girl does whatever it takes to cope. What's your point?" Lark asked sternly.

Sylvie realized she was covering herself with her arms—more out of a general defensiveness than out of embarrassment—as she stammered through a few false starts before managing, "That maybe you won't kill me? Maybe?" Lark's suspicious glare prompted her to hurry on. "I climbed up the tower and he was there in my face, and I was almost naked, and we started kissing, and...I don't know what happened or where he went, but I think that was Isaac you heard me with—please please please don't kill me." The confession might have been a profoundly dumb one, but she'd never be able to keep it from Lark. So it was either this or tuck tail and run.

Lark continued to hold Sylvie pinned with that icy glare for several long seconds. "Yeah, well, I'd guess you're safe enough," she said at last. "Anyway, it was just sex, right?"

"Yeah," Sylvie agreed readily, finding the wit to omit the addendum that it was just glorious, life-long fantasy sex.

"Not worth killing you over then, even if it was him," Lark said. "It wasn't. He'd have no call to go vanishing even if...Where did you get that shoe?"

Sylvie stared back at Lark blankly, unable to make the sudden shift in gears.

"The shoe," Lark repeated. "Where did you get that?"

"It's mine," Sylvie said. Then her brain started to catch up. "Oh. Yeah. It *isn't* local. I'm not from here either."

"You're *not* a spirit or a ghost or a...a...this?" Lark gave an expansive gesture that took in all of their surroundings. Then her jaw dropped open in comprehension. "It was you! *You* opened the new rift!"

Sylvie shook her head quickly. "I just came through it."

"But you know where it is? You can get back there?" Lark pressed her.

"Sure. Yeah," Sylvie agreed. "Do you maybe have another robe I can borrow while we talk?" Sylvie asked.

"Are you going to get me and my friends home?" Lark asked.

"Of course!" Sylvie answered sincerely. "I mean, I'll do my best."

Lark sighed, but pointed to a long black traveling cloak hanging on a hook near the fireplace. "Please try not to lose it. I like that cloak."

"How would I lose it?" Sylvie asked even as she reached for the cloak and wrapped herself in it.

"Did you come up here naked?" Lark gestured toward the single shoe Sylvie had set down on the mantle. "Did you think you'd be losing the clothes you've already lost? This tower eats clothes like a dryer eats socks. I suspect *most* of the cathedral's disused corners do."

"It does?" Sylvie cocked an eyebrow.

"Places have souls, right? At least places can develop souls. That's literally thesimancy one-o'-one," Lark said.

Sylvie nodded. That lore was established in the *Lovelace* books and, to a lesser extent, in the movies. "Any sacred site hundreds of years old is going to be humming with power and have developed a sort of life of its own." Of course that was canon in *Lovelace*, not necessarily in *Teprigoth*, but it also wasn't far removed from folk wisdom back home. Haunted houses, stone circles, graveyards, old castles, ancient ruins, ghost towns—there was a certain amount of magical thinking in how people looked at all of them.

Lark nodded. "And this isn't just any sacred site. It's a site sacred to many hundreds of years' worth of Victorian-era-level sexual repression. I think this apartment we're in was originally meant to be some sort of panic room, but it seems to have spent most of its history being used as a secret love nest for forbidden trysts. On a related note, I'm going to guess you've been harboring some sort of crush on Isaac? That's a sign of excellent taste, by the way. Don't think I'm calling you out. Anyway, the tower tapped into that and fed your fantasies back to you as a sort of spiritual manifestation of its own lustful soul. Sound about right?"

"That would...Yeah." Sylvie blushed. "Between you and me, Isaac is beyond hot, but I'd be shocked to find out he knows my face much less my name. Anyway, you're saying—"

"I'm saying that this tower is very seriously into seduction," Lark said with a smirk. "Or maybe just raw lust."

"Does the tower manifest *your* fantasies too?" Sylvie asked.

"Frequently and vigorously," Lark confessed, grinning. "More fun than getting myself off. If it was any good at pillow talk, Isaac might have some real competition. Speaking of whom, this city made us get open-minded fast about our relationship. You sleep with him? Okay. You try to take him, you're dead. Fair enough?"

"More than fair," Sylvie agreed, storing the information unexamined for later emotional evaluation. "So Isaac's actually here too? Not just some ghostly fantasy of him?"

"He is. There's four of us who've been trapped here," Lark said. "There's not a lot of residual magic for us to work with.

Most of the power gets concentrated at sites like this, so we've spread out to different bases of operation to each have our own power source while we work on getting the rift back open. It doesn't help that our wands went *poof* along with everything else we brought over. We've had to patch new ones together, and they're not the most efficient things."

"Are *all* the power sites this lusty?" Sylvie asked.

"No. But all the ones we've found that aren't lusty are downright scary," Lark said. "What's putting up with a little friendly hedonism when the alternative is blood dripping down the walls? Hang on a minute." Lark held up a hand for patience as she stepped around to the far side of the fireplace where a primitive, hand-crank telephone hung on the wall. She held the receiver to her ear. "Isaac, please." She waited for several beats. "Hey, handsome. Uh huh. Yeah. A bit more than usual, actually. Can you hold that thought? I need you to round up Holly and Amy and get them over here as soon as you can. I've got a lead on that new rift."

"Huh. I did not expect telephones," Sylvie said as Lark hung up. "I guess they make sense enough, though, when the technology level is Victorian-plus."

"Most phones aren't much more than toys here, actually," Lark said. "The physical laws aren't entirely what we're used to—like the sparse magic distribution. Steam turbines are incredibly efficient at producing energy, but electricity bleeds off at an alarming rate as it travels. Anyway, we grabbed a few of those primitive phones and rigged them up to link magically between the power sites we've claimed. *That* is working marvelously. Speak a name or ask for a conference call, and it'll patch you right through."

"I've still got like a bazillion questions," Sylvie said, "but there are clocks ticking, and I probably have people waiting on me by now, so I'd better cut straight to the uncomfortable stuff. Did you ever run into a doppelganger of yourself?"

It did seem that this was the same woman Diana had encountered on her visit to Lovelace, and Lark did a *lot* of venting about Diana and her friends barging in "to take over our lives" before Sylvie managed to calm her down again and fill her in on the whole story as she understood it. Filling Lark in did not go nearly as smoothly as it had with Alban, partly because Sylvie's Lark wasn't just a fictional character to Sylvie. She was the best friend Sylvie had never had. How do you admit to someone like that that you've been spying on the most emotionally intimate moments of their lives for the last decade? By dancing around it and downplaying it, it seemed—and re-entrenching in the personal belief that this wasn't actually a fictional character but the closest match that an exceedingly clever spell could find to that character when it went sorting through every alternate reality in the multiverse to find her.

Adding to the complexity was the fact that this wasn't even Lark's own branch of the multiverse. The tale of how that had come to pass had to be interwoven with explaining her encounter with Diana in a dialog that passed back and forth between them as each added to the other's understanding. Ultimately, it boiled down to this: uneasy with the thought that their unexplained doppelgangers could return and possibly succeed next time in a complete identity theft, Lark and her friends had worked long and hard to re-open the portal that Diana had arrived through. Once they finally succeeded, they found themselves here and not Sylvie's home world at all, as Sylvie would have expected.

What had Felicity said about this sort of thing? "When random things powered by arcane magic happen, they're almost always bad." Probably no one had ever given a moment's thought to what would happen if a fictional character proved willing and able to backtrack the intruding spell to its source. While Lark and her friends had still been trying to track down Diana and *her* friends here in Teprigoth, the gate had closed again without warning. All of their wands and other possessions had evaporated before they could get it back open, and then they'd had to spend all their time re-learning how to use magic here. Without magic they had neither a way home nor locally marketable skills, and things were looking pretty dire. Only after they figured out they needed to make wands out of conductive metals here did they start to get a handle on it.

They had also seemed to be suffering from the sort of steadily worsening delusions and paranoias Diana had reported. That had remained out of control until they'd established themselves into their sites of power and begun weaving mental protections for themselves there. The protections hadn't been a cure all. Sometimes still the insanity seemed to bleed through, but the effort had bought them some respite. At the current rate of degradation Lark figured they might still pass as reasonably sane for a couple more years, but there was no pretending they could hold out forever.

By the time they'd hashed out that much of what had happened, they agreed they'd best get moving to meet Sylvie's friends at the archives. Lark excused herself to the next room to get dressed for going out. "Did you need to borrow an actual dress?" Lark offered through the door she'd left ajar.

"Depends on how we're getting to the archives," Sylvie said. "I've got clothes waiting there. Can we just use the stairs? I'm only starting on this magic stuff, and I couldn't fly even if I had a wand. I climbed up the outside of the cathedral, but it took too much out of me to feel safe about going back down."

"I took out part of the stairs down to keep people from coming up," Lark said. "I'll fly us down."

Yes! Sylvie exulted silently with a double fist pump. This was a whole magnitude better than a talking cat. She was about to go *flying* with the *real* Lark Starling. No one would ever believe her. She could capture the whole thing on video and everyone would say it was Hollywood magic.

"I prefer flying at night so I won't get seen but I think the fog is thick enough today if we're careful," Lark said. "Hey! Would you get the phone?"

Sylvie found the casual question a bit of a puzzler. She hadn't heard the phone ring, but she picked up the earpiece. It was just dead air. "Hello?" Nothing. Feeling foolish she re-examined the request and decided it had been to literally "get the phone" and bring it to Lark. Sylvie looked to see if she could detach the phone from the wall, but even powered by magic, the thing was still apparently attached to a land line that ran down through a hole in the floorboards. "Hello?" she tried again.

Lark emerged from the bedroom in her petticoats, still securing her corset, and took the receiver out of Sylvie's hand with a grateful smile. "Hey, Isaac. Yeah. That was just the lead I was talking about. Her name's Sylvie. I'll explain when you get here. Well, just come on over when you find her. If we're not here we'll be down in the cathedral archives. Love you too. Bye." Lark turned back to Sylvie as she hung up the phone. "Holly's not answering. Probably got errands this morning. How did anyone ever build a civilization calling over land lines? Anyway, let's go meet your friends."

"I...couldn't hear him," Sylvie said.

"You're the first strange voice he's ever heard over that phone," Lark assured her. "He was just trying to figure out what the heck was going on. Thanks for grabbing the call anyway."

"Yeah. Sure." Sylvie bit her lip. "Do you mind if I try something?" Lark shrugged, so Sylvie picked up the receiver again. "Issac, please," she said, mimicking Lark's original call as best she could. She waited through a good fifteen seconds of dead air.

Lark shrugged again. "Guess the magic's not attuned to you. You did say you're new at this." She took charge of the phone again. "Isaac, please." A couple of seconds ticked bye. "Yeah, it's me again. Just can't stay away. If it's convenient on the way here, could you pick us up a couple of bottles of Fena Rosada? With luck we'll never be able to get it again, and I want to be able to celebrate."

"Can I try one more experiment?" Sylvie asked.

"You're not going to ask me to excuse another call to Isaac, are you?" Lark chuckled.

Sylvie shook her head. A couple of theories were competing in her head, and she really, *really* didn't like one of them. With the fresh lesson of unexpected magical consequences in mind, she picked up the phone and gave it one last try. "Arthur, please."

"Hello?"

"Hey, Isaac. This is Sylvie," she said, smiling in relief and giving Lark a nod. The last thing she'd wanted was to have to sort out if all of Lark's friends here were some sort of hallucination. "I just wanted to say hi for myself and make sure I'd figured this phone out."

"I, uh...think you misdialed," he said.

"I'm Lark's friend," Sylvie said. "The 'lead' she just mentioned."

The phone went silent for several seconds. "Are you trying to be funny, or do you need help?"

"I...Arthur?" Sylvie asked hesitantly. "Is this Arthur Allen?"

"So you do need help?" he asked.

"Please tell me," she begged quietly. "Diana thinks you're dead. She told me you were dead."

"Who *is* this?" he demanded.

"My name is Sylvie like I said. You don't know me but I know Diana. You sound just like Arthur, and she'll kill me if it turns out you are and I didn't tell her. Please?"

"Why did you call me?"

"Such a long story. Please?" Please are you the man whose ghost I just made love to in my fantasies come to life? Please can there be a happily-ever-after for my new friend Diana?

Please can I have my teenage hopes back of watching Isaac's adventures go on and on? So many questions she couldn't actually ask rolled into that one little word, and any one alone could have been responsible for the tears on her cheeks.

Interminable seconds ticked by in silence. "This is Arthur."

"Thank you!" The tears weren't stopping. "You're alive?"

"I...don't think so."

Sylvie's heart went cold. "Okay, I asked for that, but it's not funny."

"Sorry. I...just don't know what else to tell you," Arthur's voice said. "I'm trying to figure this out myself."

Sylvie found she was biting her thumb and it was starting to get painful. "Where *are* you?" she asked after finally managing to unclench her jaw.

"Tell Diana not to worry about me, okay? I think I'm safe," the voice said. "It's Martin that needs help."

"We're already trying to find him," Sylvie said unsteadily.

"He's trapped. He's lost. Something's stalking him."

"Where *is* he?" Sylvie was still crying, and there was no keeping it out of her voice. But she'd couldn't keep track any more of which bits of what was happening were responsible. It didn't matter anyway. She'd been left talking to dead air.

"Haven't a clue what that was about," Lark said, holding out a full wine glass that she'd produced from somewhere while Sylvie was on the phone, "but do you drink?"

CHAPTER EIGHT
DESCENT

"Where *is* everybody?!" Sylvie demanded.

"Sssh," Wambleesha scolded quietly. "Books."

"This is all of us," Brian said, holding out a page torn from a hotel notepad.

Martin spotted but on the move, the hastily scrawled note read. *Catching 4:10 train at Bothwell Station. If you're not there will see you when we get back.*

Sylvie checked her watch. The rendezvous had come and gone.

"Hey, at least you've got Diana's autograph," Brian said, cheerily pointing to the signature on the note before doing a double take to stare at Lark.

"That's not Diana Taylor," Sylvie said, failing to suppress a grin. "Brian Larson, meet Lark Starling."

"I'm told you know me. Creepy, really, but I'll try not to hold it against you," Lark said with a little smile.

"*Please* tell me this hasn't all be some Rube Goldberg setup for a cheesy hidden camera moment," Brian sighed.

"I'm not in on the joke if it is," Lark assured him. "If it helps, you don't have to believe in me or even call me Lark. I'll answer to pronouns just fine."

The flight down hadn't been everything Sylvie had imagined it would. The phone call had left her in a mood, and Lark wanted to stick close to the tower anyway to avoid any risk of straying too far from her source of power and having the spell cut out on them. She'd just waved her coppery wand and lowered them almost straight down as if they'd stepped together into an invisible elevator.

Waiting inside the archives they'd found only Wambleesha, Brian, Ettie, and Alban. Apparently Ettie had suggested rounding Alban up when they'd failed to find any of the others. Sylvie wasn't unhappy to see him, but she *was* worried about how she was going to deal with being in one room with both him and Brian. For the moment she just kept her distance from both and tried to stay focused on business.

"All right," she said toward that end. "Lark is who I expected I'd have found when you came back from fetching Diana. And since I was right about that part, I'm pretty sure that the man Diana's gone chasing is Eli Canon, not Martin Kight."

"I'm really sorry to break it to you," Lark sighed, "but Eli's dead. He died right here in the archives."

"He did?" Wambleesha asked, alarmed. "Who's Eli?"

"In my world he's the fictional character Martin plays," Sylvie explained before asking Lark, "Where's his body?"

"There wasn't anything left to bury," Lark answered coldly. "He got caught in the crossfire of some sort of magical duel down in the archives while we were still trying to find our doppelgangers. There were some seriously heavy-duty spells flying around."

"There you go then. Eli's alive," Sylvie said confidently. "Look," she went on in response to the dubious stares that had earned her, "back home I'm nothing special, but it turns out while I'm here I've basically got psychic powers. The way my mind works there's stuff I just know. Climbing to the top of that tower thinking I'd find *the* Lark Starling was insane, but I knew before I started that's exactly who I'd find. Now I know that Eli's alive and Diana's chasing him, but we're not supposed to join. The real Martin Kight's been here as long as Lark has, and he needs help. We're supposed to find Martin and bring him home."

"Okay." Wambleesha nodded. "Sure. Which one's Martin again?"

"I'm kind of with her," Alban said, pointing at Wambleesha. "Finding someone who's lost sounds like a good plan, but I need a play bill or something to keep track of what's going on."

"And I'm still not sold on this whole 'cast of characters' you're laying out," Brian said. "I'm barely taking it on faith the Lark is Lark and not Diana. Where does this 'Martin is Eli' even come from? 'Diana is to Lark as Martin is to Eli' is an answer on an I.Q. test, not some sort of magical prediction."

"I think I know how to prove this," Sylvie said. "Lark, can you do that photo-print spell of yours here with your current wand?"

"Yeah." Lark nodded. "It always comes out sepia-tone, though."

"Good enough. The rest of you stay here." She led Lark out of earshot. When they returned, Sylvie laid out the collection of half-a-dozen photographs Lark had conjured on the nearest reading table. "Wam..." she started, but she couldn't manage to recall the archivist's full name and just beckoned to her instead. "Is one of these the man you've seen downstairs?"

Wambleesha spent about three seconds looking over the head shots of six of Lark's old classmates before picking up one and handing it to Sylvie. "That's him."

"Ladies and gentlemen," Sylvie said, holding up the photo of Eli/Martin for the others to see, "I give you the phantom of the archives."

Wambleesha led the way down the long central aisle between shelves of books that just went on and on, illuminated by the steady, yellow glow of the big brass flashlight that—in fine, faux-British fashion—she called a torch. In theory, there were overhead lights they could be using instead, but when they'd reached the second sub-basement and she'd thrown the switch they hadn't offered up a single spark or flicker. "Some addle pate comes down and leaves them running," she'd sighed. "The cathedral's generator can't keep them powered this far away, so they run on batteries. When you find any lights that'll still turn on, be sure to turn them off after you," she added sternly. Then she'd gone to find a couple of backup batteries and what flashlights she could lay her hands on.

Rather than immediately replace any batteries, she'd started right in with a flashlight. Her stated plan was to save the batteries for the walk back, when she'd be replacing the farthest ones out that needed it and not have to make that whole trip twice. "There's supposed to be a maintenance robot that handles this, but I haven't seen it in months," she complained. "The fool thing probably let its own steam generator *and* its battery run dry. I'll never find it in here."

Whatever had become of the robot in question, other mechanical creatures scurried by on spider-like legs or trundled by on tank-like treads with some regularity. The treaded robots hauled large cargoes of books or—occasionally and curiously—rocks with them while the smaller spidery ones shelved and unshelved the books, climbing as necessary to reach their goals.

"Doing a little reorganizing?" Brian asked, noting the scope of the effort the robots seemed to be collectively putting in.

"Always," Wambleesha said. "The city's too crowded to expand to the sides, there's limits to how high we can build, and the collection of records is always growing. It's illegal to throw anything out. So there's robots digging a brand new sub-basement below us right now. The newer a document is the more likely someone will want to see it, so each time a new level is finished the shelving robots start moving things down to make room upstairs for the incoming documents."

"So you have really advanced robots but no electronic document storage?" Brian asked, puzzled.

"We're *supposed* to have the lights," Wambleesha pointed out.

"That's not...Sorry. Never mind," Brian sighed. He exchanged glances with Sylvie, who simply nodded. Either this was all just some sort of magical virtual-reality facade that didn't need to make sense, or it was a universe specifically picked for having its own physical laws and social circumstances that had somehow combined to produce the same appearance as that facade. Nothing here was required to live up to their mundane expectations, even as everything conspired to live up to narrative expectations.

So long as they remained on this side of the bridge, Sylvie realized, she was going to become more and more reliant on her understanding of narrative conventions over what passed for common sense back home. That could get tricky, constantly switching back and forth between the two very different sets of expectations if the pattern held in other worlds as well. Then there was the danger that the longer they interacted with a world, the more it would shift from fitting narrative logic toward fitting common sense. If these *were* real worlds and not virtual realities, they'd have to. The harsh logistics of everyday life would eventually have to overwhelm even the most stubborn and compelling of fictional conceits. That was sort of their job.

"So how deep do the archives go then?" Ettie asked.

"I've been down as far as sub-basement one-hundred and seventy-four," Wambleesha said. "I think. The deeper you go, the more disorganized it gets. Robots aren't that great without human supervision, but no one's willing to supervise them down there anymore. They've been left to their own devices for centuries."

"So the question isn't, 'How does someone get lost for months down here?'," Brian said, "It's, 'How does someone get lost for months down here and survive?'"

"Yeah," Wambleesha agreed.

"How sure are we he's still alive?" Alban asked.

"Pretty sure," Sylvie said. She couldn't actually rule out that the narrative purpose of looking for Martin was to find something he'd done or discovered rather than to bring him back alive. Her ability to predict would be limited unless threads of meaning strongly converged. Encountering inverted tropes would surely be a hazard as well, and the surest way to lose sight of the narrative threads would be to get cocky. Every in-character prediction made within a story as if it was indisputable fact was really just an invitation for the character to get the rug pulled out from under her. "How long has it been since you've heard him?" she asked Wambleesha.

"I had to find some documents on sub-basement thirteen last week," Wambleesha said. "I think it was him I heard then. It's where we should start looking."

"Thirteen?" Brian remarked. "Well, that bodes."

"It's safe enough," Wambleesha said. "The books are still friendly, and the lights may be working there. If you get lost, keep your hand on one wall and always go up when you can, never down. You'll be all right."

"There are unfriendly books?" Ettie asked, clearly unsure whether she should be doubtful or alarmed.

"Down where nobody visits the books have gone feral," Wambleesha said. "They growl at me. I don't like it."

"What *really* bodes," said Lark, who had seemed lost in her own thoughts for some time, "is the deeper we go, the more concentrated the magic gets. I'd expected the seat of the cathedral's soul to be somewhere near the altar, but we've been getting closer to it, not farther from it. I'm not seeing how that makes sense if the deeper you go, the fewer people have ever set foot there."

In answer, Wambleesha pulled a book at random off the nearest shelf and opened it to the minutes of a ward council meeting from several years before. She read aloud a dry and boring passage before re-shelving it. "Books remember," she said with finality. "It's what they do. You've already forgotten what I just said, but the book will still tell you word for word a hundred years from now. A book can absorb and trap echoes better than a floor or a wall or...anything, and books don't forget just because a robot puts them on a different shelf. The soul of the cathedral moves with the books."

"Oh...my..." Lark stopped in her tracks with her jaw hanging open. "You know what? This is a bad idea. This is a spectacularly bad idea. Sylvie, your friend is happy. Let's leave him to it."

"He's dying, Lark," Sylvie said firmly. "His brain is coming apart piece by piece, probably as fast as yours ever was. He may already be certifiable. The Lark Starling I know wouldn't need any more than that to charge in headlong to the rescue because she wants to live in a world where magic is something more than a power hoarded by mega-corporations and secret political cabals. Are you that woman, or aren't you?"

"I'm not some two-dimensional movie character if that's what you mean," Lark responded hotly.

"No," Sylvie agreed calmly. "But Diana's spell went searching for all the best parts of that character and found them in you. I know I'm not wrong that you want your magic to be meant for something better. This is one of those chances."

Lark sighed. "This isn't just about me. All the centers of power in this city are either lusty or murderous. *All of them.* If we're lucky, what we're searching for down here is the island of the Lotus-Eaters. If we find it, we won't come back because we won't want to. If we're unlucky, there's a dark heart lurking down there with the 'feral books'. If we find it, we won't come back because we won't be able to. Either way, this is no evening's stroll down to see if your friend's hanging out in the subway tunnels. We need to back out *now,* think about what we're getting into, and come back prepared if we come back at all."

"Sub-basement thirteen wouldn't hurt you," Wambleesha insisted. "It's nice."

"Does it eat your clothes?" Lark demanded.

Wambleesha turned a visibly bright red even in the dim light. "Only sometimes," she mumbled, looking at her feet. "When I'm careless."

"I am now confused, concerned, *and* intrigued," Alban admitted.

"You would be." Ettie rolled her eyes at him, but seemed more amused than anything.

"Okay. Yeah. What's this about eating clothes?" Brian asked.

Lark offered a brief and, in places, more delicately phrased recounting of what she'd already shared with Sylvie about the soul of the cathedral and its feedback of fantasies. "I have a hard enough time keeping perspective up there," she finished, jabbing a thumb toward the ceiling. "If it gets more intense down here, I really don't have a plan on how to cope."

"It's not—" Wambleesha began.

"By the time we catch up with Sylvie's friend it will be," Lark insisted. "Or do you really think he's just been down there wandering around all this time without thinking, 'Hey, why don't I try going up?'"

"This is your friend, Sylvie," Alban said. "If you—"

"No. Wait," Sylvie stopped him. "First, he's not really my friend. Second, Lark is making perfect sense—but I feel I've proved that when this world bridge gets involved it drops us into skewed situations that defy probability. I don't know if it keeps influencing things after we arrive, but I do know it loads the dice before the game begins. So let's compromise. Let's hook up one of these batteries, sit down with some light, and talk things out right here before we decide we need to go trekking back upstairs. How does that sound?"

They did. Curled up on the cool stone floor between bookshelves in what had quickly become a cheerily lit library, they talked logistics and timetables and theories, available information and available resources. In the end, Lark admitted that the only thing to gain by delaying was to go back and pack a lunch and some water, maybe some camping equipment. Even if things came to a fight, Lark had her wand, Alban and Ettie each admitted to a concealed blade and a concealed, derringer-like holdout pistol, and Sylvie had her arsenal. None of them really wanted more. Brian had never had any more practical training than a few rounds of laser tag, and Wambleesha wasn't sure she'd know which end of a gun to hold, so even if they'd had weapons there were limits to what good it would do them.

Much more serious a concern, everyone agreed, was that the place was expansive enough it might take them days to find Martin. To that Sylvie argued, "We've already come this far. Let's *try* going down and looking where Wambleesha says she heard him last. She vouches that it's not going to get bloody and that we won't get lost, and it's our one realistic chance to find him quickly. We look around down there for a couple of hours. I'll even set a two-hour alarm on my phone. If we don't find him by the time it goes off, we admit this is a long-term project. We resurface, we try to make contact with Diana, and any of us who return come armed like we're about to set off on a week-long spelunking expedition and with whatever magical preparations we can think of. No matter what happens tonight, we don't let anything lure us lower than sub-basement thirteen. Does that work for everybody?"

That plan eventually met with murmurs of acceptance. "Just one more thing then," Sylvie said, singling out Brian. "You. With me. We need to talk before I can let you do this."

Together they walked back the way they'd come until the sound of the others trying to pry more useful information about the archives out of Wambleesha had become unintelligible in the distance. Sylvie drew a bracing breath, caught Brian's worried look, and tried to cudgel her brain into finding a decent way to start this conversation. Brian beat her to it. "Okay. Yeah. I'm sorry," he said with a sigh.

"You're...sorry?" No version that she'd rehearsed in her head had started the conversation anything like this.

"Yeah." He massaged his forehead tiredly. "I don't know what more I can say. I knew I had to tell you, I just figured it could wait until we got back to the hotel. My poker face is even worse than I thought."

"Tell me...what?" Sylvie asked warily.

Brian paused, considering her. "That's *not* what this is about?"

"It is now!" she assured him. "Spill."

"I, uh...I 'slept' with Ettie. I know, you warned me what it would be like here, but...Anyway, we got to flirting on the way back to the hotel, and the next thing I knew we were making out in an alley. Then...Okay, you don't need the details. Sorry."

He cringed at the expression on her face. "Yeah. I'll just find my way back to—"

"No! Wait! Brian, I'm not angry. I..." Words. Where were the words? She gave up, grabbed him by the collar, and pulled him into a kiss. She wasn't sure this was fair. She'd kissed him when they'd been dating, but never this sort of forceful shut-up-and-just-be kiss. By all but the most technical interpretations it was breaking new ground with him. She also let it linger a lot longer than was really necessary just to break the conversational momentum. She'd offer to pay him some sort of forfeit later if he insisted she'd cheated.

"It's okay," she said, locking eyes with him. "And I think I needed to do that before *my* confession that I've been with Alban, too. That's what I had to tell you before I could let you get any deeper into this with me. If that upsets you then you should go on back to the hotel because I *don't* feel guilty about it. I won't call you a hypocrite, and we can talk about it if you want when I get back, but I don't think it's fair to you or safe for any of us to take risks down here together while you're upset with me. I hope you're not angry, but I'll take what's coming if you are."

"I..." He stopped talking almost before he'd started, clearly working to deal with something.

"Don't worry whether it makes sense to be angry with me," she prodded him. She knew him well enough to know that was part of what was going on in there. He was studying law and it wasn't for the sake of a big corporate paycheck. Carefully considered justice was one of his things. "Emotions don't have to make sense. They just are. Experience them now, dissect them later."

Brian slumped down against the end of a bookshelf, his expression still unreadable.

"So here's the thing I've been thinking about since this morning," she said. "I'm not giving up magic. I'm not giving up exploring these worlds. That means I'm going to get tempted over and over and over and over. Sometimes I'm going to give in. I refuse to apologize for that or to let it turn into a dark, dreadful secret. Apparently the thought of an actual relationship with people from one of these worlds is a complete non-starter, though, for all sorts of reasons. Also, I really, *really* like guys. I want an actual relationship with one for all sorts of reasons, but I can't just start initiating every interesting man into the world of magic and hope it works out any more than I could hide this side of my life from them. That leaves a pool of three men I could turn to. One of those is almost certainly dead. One of them is lost, trapped, and possibly insane even if we find him.

"That kind of leaves you, Brian, and I really like you. I'm not in love with you, but I'm starting to think maybe I could wind up there. So I'd be a royal idiot not to give this relationship thing a try if you'll have me on those terms. You're right that I've got a 'world-hopping test' now. It's more important than the roller coaster test. If coming with me to L.A. is what you *really* want after we get home then, yeah, we should talk about that. Even if you walk away right now because you need time to think about it, we can still talk about it later. I owe us both that much at least. You've always been a good friend, even when I didn't deserve it."

She drew a deep breath, feeling exhausted now that she'd got all that out. When he remained silent and unreadable, she went on. "I want to say, 'Don't leave me hanging here,' but I know that's a lot to ask. So I'll give you like a minute to figure out some words, and if they aren't there I'll go call off this expedition so we can make sure you wind up safe back at the hotel."

"This is cheating," he said at last.

"You're not wrong," she agreed. "You want me to walk back across that line and pretend I never said anything?"

"No," he said. At last, he took a long breath and looked up to meet her gaze. "So what you're saying is I could maybe have you and you'd still be okay with me sleeping with other amazing women who'd barely notice me back home because you know for a fact they're going to be casual flings? That's a lot to take in, but it doesn't sound like there's much of a down side." He managed a shaky smile.

"Except that I'd need you to reciprocate, yes." She nodded. "Neither of us gets to commit to any of that right now, but if we can't accept that as a possible future, facing unknown magic together beside the people we just slept with is going to turn awful at best."

"There was also the bit about clothes going missing down here," Brian said, looking more animated.

"You sound almost like you'd consider that a plus." Sylvie grinned.

"The odds are in my favor," he chuckled. "Even our little archivist is really cute, and seeing you nude never got taken off my bucket list when we stopped dating."

"And maybe Lark Starling will get naked?" she asked, eyebrow cocked in amusement.

"And maybe Lark Starling will get naked," Brian said. "The future remains hazy, but you make a compelling argument."

"There's no chance of there being an 'us' in this mess if we can't be honest about finding other people attractive," she said with a smile.

"Life gets weird fast," he laughed.

"It does that," Sylvie said.

"Has no one here ever heard of a stairwell?" Brian asked. "You know, where you descend several floors down a single shaft instead of all this wandering around to find each new stair? Or an elevator? How can we have dexterous, independent spider bots but not a lousy elevator?"

"Maybe it's a *feng shui* thing," Sylvie offered, but the original novelty of exploration had worn off about five floors up, and now she was getting sick of it herself.

"Historical preservation," Wambleesha said. "We're not allowed to renovate, just expand down and move books."

"But if most of this was built by robots, they should have had the elevator technology all along! Besides, who would even *know* if you added an elevator?!" Brian asked in exasperation. "It's not like you have to hire contractors. These robots can construct and reinforce finished stonework; at a minimum they could make a proper stairwell if someone just told them to do it."

"What do you mean?" Ettie asked, blinking.

"Reprogram the robots," Brian reiterated. "Give them new instructions."

Wambleesha giggled.

"What?" Brian demanded.

"Robots don't listen," Wambleesha said. "They're not books, silly."

"If you have robots," Brian persisted, "someone programmed them. Someone can reprogram them."

"I think we're hitting one of those translation barriers again," Alban said.

"How can programming a robot be a foreign concept?!" Of all of them, Brian was clearly the least accustomed to lengthy hikes, and his nerves were starting to fray as his energy flagged.

"The robots show up. They do their jobs," Ettie said. "That's it. That's robots."

"There's not even a management department at the ward level," Wambleesha said.

"Oh. Okay," Brian said, finally accepting the answer. "Government monopoly."

"I'm not convinced there's a management department anywhere," Lark said. "The bureaucracy in this city is insane. Everything's so opaque I'm amazed it has functional services of any kind."

"Hey," Sylvie said. "Does anyone else smell that?"

Everyone stopped. "Incense?" Ettie asked. It certainly wasn't the background vanilla scent that permeated the archives.

"I was going to guess 'Christmas tree'," Lark said, "but yours sounds more dramatic."

Wambleesha pulled a book off the near shelf and began leafing through it, peering intently through her spectacles. "He's near," she concluded as she snapped the book shut and replaced it on the shelf. Most of the company looked at her askance, and even Sylvie waffled back and forth briefly over whether that was insanity or a misunderstood gift before finally deciding she'd just need to guardedly keep an open mind.

"We're still just on eleven, aren't we?" Sylvie asked.

Wambleesha nodded. "I've sometimes heard him as far up as seven, though."

"Has...anyone ever been with you when you met him?" Ettie asked.

"Wait. I think she's right," Alban said, cocking his head as if to listen. "Something's changed, anyway."

"Oh, hey, Diana." They all instinctively swung their lights around to fall on the chiseled, movie-star jaw of Martin Kight, his jaw covered with no more than a couple of days' stubble and his hair only mildly unkempt despite his supposed months down here in isolation. Martin sat with his back against a wall and a book in his lap as if he'd been reading in the pitch black. He threw up his arm to ward off the sudden brilliance. "Are we doing steampunk now?" The placement of the large book made it hard to say definitively, but Martin might very well be naked.

"Just a quick check...Is this anyone's fantasy?" Sylvie asked. Truth to tell, it could have been one of her own, though it had been a while since she'd revisited any of those. The abs alone certainly could have qualified, though the actor's bad boy appeal hadn't had the enduring effect on her psyche that Arthur's character, Isaac, had.

"I dunno," Martin laughed. "I preferred the whole retro sci-fi aesthetic with those little tunic dresses, but I can work with a Victorian change of pace." He clapped the book closed and climbed to his feet. Yes, he was naked. His body also proved a reasonable match for Sylvie's teenage imagination. That was at once nice, because she'd liked her imaginings, and disturbing, because it cast further doubt on whether this might be the cathedral itself instead of Martin.

"Of course, we could try this whole 'Arabian Nights' theme if your friends are into it," Martin added, presenting the cover of the book. It bore an elaborate, colorful illustration that might have been inspired by the tales of Scheherazade.

"Ummm...Martin, do you have pants around here somewhere?" Brian asked. Apparently he felt the dice hadn't been weighted enough in his favor for this particular game after all.

Martin glanced over each of his shoulders in turn, to no avail. "Somewhere," he concluded. "Nothing Arabian, though. You're right. We'll come back to that." He slid the book into an open spot on the shelf.

"Oh, dear," Wambleesha sighed. "This is all *supposed* to be city records, but sometimes little treasures get slipped into the collection. Can we all just pretend we didn't see that? They keep the job much more interesting."

"Sure," Lark agreed before turning her attention back to Martin. "Come on, friend. The others are upstairs waiting on you. I'm sure you won't need pants."

"How do we know he's real?" Sylvie pressed, her gaze swinging back and forth between Lark and Wambleesha when it wasn't being drawn back to Martin. Her meager experience with that one apparition likely paled in comparison to what either of them had experienced here.

"Martin, are you real?" Lark asked.

"Think so," he said, pondering. "Why?"

"It's more convenient if you are," Lark said. "Simplest way to be sure is if we move the party upstairs, okay?"

"Where's my costume?" he asked. "I can't play steampunk without a costume."

"We'll find you one upstairs," Lark said patiently.

Alban moved to shrug out of his coat, but it had barely cleared his shoulders before Ettie gave him a gentle swat. "Don't you dare," she whispered just loud enough for Sylvie to hear.

"Here," Sylvie said, trying to keep a straight face as she doffed the bowler hat that had been part of her original costume. It had survived this far by virtue of having been left with her dress for the climb.

"Excellent," Martin said, accepting the hat. "Where's the goggles? I'm sure there's supposed to be goggles."

"How about a spyglass?" Sylvie asked after a quick search of the tools on her belt. The more modest dress she'd donned for this expedition had made strapping equipment onto her thighs nearly pointless and the little waistcoat that had come with it lacked any useful pockets. She'd transferred the crucial items from her arsenal onto her belt and her single arm strap but had wound up leaving all the purely decorative stuff and a few other odds and ends back at the hotel.

"Capital!" Martin said, accepting the spyglass too. "That's more in-character than 'excellent', isn't it? 'Capital'?"

"I'm sure," Sylvie agreed.

"Right, then. What's the conflict? What's my motivation?" Martin asked.

"Ummm...Racing up the jungle mountain to be the first to reach the lost city of...Uplantis?" Sylvie offered.

"Your world is weird," Wambleesha said.

"You've no idea," Sylvie assured her.

CHAPTER NINE
Something Wicked

"That can't be good," Sylvie said, shining her phone light up at the silvery mist pouring slowly, fluidly down the stairway in front of them to spread out across the floor of the gallery. They'd made it back as far as sub-basement eight and nearly to the next stairway up before they'd found themselves walking through the eerie, ankle-deep mist. The top of the stairs had been enveloped entirely in the fog, obscuring everything. It could have been Sylvie's imagination, but she thought she heard a giggle like the ones she'd heard while she was climbing the cathedral.

"No. It's okay," Wambleesha assured her. "It never damages the books."

"You get this a lot?" Brian asked dubiously.

"Yes," Wambleesha said. "Well, some. It's an invitation."

"An invitation to what?" Alban asked.

"To play," Wambleesha said.

"I think we just found the lotus eaters," Lark said.

"They're harmless," Wambleesha insisted. "Except for the clothes," she added with a blush.

"Whoa! Hold on, tiger," Ettie said, grabbing Martin's arm as he started up the stairs. "Let's not rush into anything."

"What?" Martin responded indignantly. "Aren't we playing?"

"Of course we are," a young woman giggled, appearing out of the fog at the top of the stair. She was blond. She was busty. She was dressed all in black lace—or, rather, black lace was all she was dressed in. Her outfit consisted mostly of petticoats, a corset she was one deep breath away from spilling out of, and a flimsy robe so sheer it wouldn't have hidden anything even if it wasn't hanging fully open.

"Okay," Sylvie murmured. "This one's not *my* fantasy."

"Hey, Hannah!" Martin called brightly. "Are you playing the Queen of Uplantis?"

"Whatever you want, angel." The woman smiled radiantly, mist swirling around her bare feet as she casually descended a few steps. "Are these my princesses?"

"We're all just passing through," Lark said curtly. "No time for games today."

"There's *always* time for games," Hannah sighed, not quite spilling out of the corset but coming close enough to have earned a short-lived censor bar on basic cable. "The world will still be there waiting when we're ready."

"It doesn't wait," Lark insisted. "It keeps moving and half of us are running low on time, including your little angel." She nodded toward Martin.

"Go if you must." Hannah waved a hand dismissively. "No one's keeping you. But my angel stays. It's not safe for you up there, is it angel?"

"It is now," Sylvie said. "I can take him home. He needs to heal. He's not well."

"I *am* home," Martin insisted. "I'm safe. I've got friends to play with. Have you *seen* the monsters out there?"

"Lotus," Lark coughed into the back of her hand.

"Look," Sylvie said, "Martin can heal, then he can come back. No one's going to hold him once he's better. But he *needs to get better*. If you *are* his friend you'll understand."

"Did I mention monsters?" Martin asked.

"We can take you straight to the bridge and then home," Brian said. "There won't be any time for monsters."

"You're already putting him in danger," Hannah said evenly. "There's not enough power up here to mask his scent. She's sniffing around, looking for him."

"Who is?" Sylvie demanded.

From back in the darkness behind them a sound erupted that mixed all the cheeriest qualities of a howling wolf with the legendary shriek of nails across a chalkboard.

"That is!" Martin said, clearly ready to bolt and run just as soon as he could decide on a direction, but Ettie kept a firm grip on his arm.

Hannah appeared to mutter some unladylike imprecation, though it was quiet enough to be drowned out by the nerve-rattling howl. "See? She already knows he's up here. You've got to take him back down."

Sylvie didn't wait for Martin or anyone else to decide where to go. There really was only one direction under the circumstances. Grabbing his wrist, she yanked him toward the stairs—and he offered no real resistance. "Too late," she brusquely told Hannah as she pushed past the woman. "If you can't hide him up here you can't get him down past...her...either."

"There's other stairs!" Hannah protested.

"No," Sylvie said coldly as they brushed past Hannah. "He comes with us. You can help, you can get in the way, or you can get out of the way. Up to you." When she glanced back over her shoulder the others were running up the stairs after them, but Hannah had vanished along with the fog flowing past their feet.

"So who or what's back there?" Sylvie demanded again of Martin.

"Ask Diana," he said, glowering at Lark. "It was *her* bright idea."

"I'm asking *you*," Sylvie pressed, getting in his face as they reached the top of the stairs. The others came hurrying past to shuffle Wambleesha forward again to lead the way.

"We could've left Bijou be," Martin said, "but *no*! Di had to get all Count of Monte Cristo. You think she *cared* about the people here?! She just wanted her revenge."

"What are you babbling about? Is that...Bijou down there?" Sylvie asked.

Martin shook his head. "We tossed Bijou through the gates of hell all right. But when we did, something came out."

While Sylvie was still processing that remark, Brian grabbed her hand, Ettie grabbed Martin's, and they both got dragged unceremoniously into a run. They'd barely made it into the next gallery before the shrieking howl sounded again, unmistakably closer. Too much closer.

"If you let something crawl in from hell, what's it doing lurking in a cathedral?!" Brian demanded. "I mean, demon? Holy site? How?"

"Catholic demon," Lark said. Of them all she wasn't the least bit winded, as she'd already levitated a couple of inches off the ground with a flick of her wand, and was floating easily alongside them. "Teprian cathedral. Yeah, they're monotheists here but the similarities are superficial. Every bit of it's blasphemy as far as Dante would be concerned."

"Can you fly out of here with Martin and...the archivist?" Sylvie said, finding it even harder to remember the woman's name under pressure. "If this thing's chasing Martin we can just get out of the way and catch up later."

"If," Lark agreed. "Then again, what do these 'intuitions' of yours tell you about splitting up right now?"

"Oh." Sylvie blanched at the thought of what she'd just suggested. She'd nearly panicked into thinking rationally instead of narratively. Luckily, Lark seemed to have caught on, too. She probably needed to clue everyone in at first chance rather than continue to hoard the knowledge. "Right. Bad idea. Can you fly *all* of us out of here? Or wall off a stairway?" She wasn't having much trouble talking, either. Keeping up with what the others considered a run amounted to more of an easy jog for her.

"Can't fly more than a couple of you at a time, but the stairway's a good bottleneck." Lark grabbed Brian's arm and he nearly stumbled before he realized his feet were no longer touching the floor, then she slipped her wand into its belt sheath and shifted ahead to grab Martin, too. "Catch your breath," she told them. "Everyone else, put some speed on. I'll let you breathe in turns, but Sylvie's right. I should have stopped and tried something before we left the last stair behind, but going back's a waste. We need to reach that next stair."

Lark coasted alongside the four runners for half a minute or so before darting ahead a short distance, dropping her passengers off, and returning for Wambleesha and Ettie.

"Gotta admit this is not how I imagined the day would go," Alban told Sylvie with a rueful grin just before the awful howl sounded again.

"At least it's not you she's after," Sylvie said. She was still keeping up with him easily, but he was showing good stamina and they put on a little extra speed to close the distance with the others.

"Doesn't matter, does it?" Alban asked. "If we're in a story, only the people who stick together stand a chance."

"I don't think we're actually in a —" Sylvie objected.

"But that's the pattern, isn't it? I've read plenty of cheap novels. That's how you knew about Lark, about Martin. That's why we shouldn't split up. We can argue about why the rules are in play, but they *are* in play, aren't they?"

"Yeah," Sylvie admitted. "I think they are. But what kind of story and who's the hero?" She noticed he had his little derringer-like pistol in hand. "Think that'll do any good?" she asked, nodding to it.

"Probably not," he said. "A long shot's better than no shot." Then they both shut up and saved their breath for running, trying not to think too hard about all the potentially lethal unknowns they were being forced to deal with.

Even with those boosts from Lark, they were steadily losing ground to the alleged demon much too quickly for comfort. There was no judging how far away it might be either, given they'd no idea of the "normal" volume of a fiendish howl. That uncertainty was nerve-wracking all by itself. With each shriek Sylvie could feel it tear at the credulous confidence that had been letting her take so much in stride up to now. Without the security-blanket-like presence of Lark hovering there beside them it would certainly already have cracked.

Somehow they made it to that next stairway up without their unsettling pursuer coming into sight, and they clattered up it in a rush. "Stand back," Lark warned as they reached the top. She waved her wand. Wambleesha shrieked in dismay as an entire bookshelf began to rise off the floor, teetering ominously.

"No no no no no!" the archivist cried, but the bookshelf came thudding down across the top of the stairway. She seemed slightly mollified that it had landed face up, the entire collection of books still safely corralled—but only slightly.

"Sorry," Lark said, "but we're running out of options." Another bookcase came thudding down on top of the first, then another and another. "That ought to buy us some time," she said. "Come on." It also helped by muffling the howls. That might have been the best part.

They hadn't gone ten paces before something slammed into the bookcases from below, hard enough to make them all shudder. A blue-tinted hand with nails like claws wedged its way up through a narrow crack between the shelves and the stairway wall. Suddenly Ettie was there, slamming a stiletto blade deep into the hand and eliciting an inhuman shriek from its owner. The hand hastily withdrew, snapping the blade of the stiletto in the process. The part that clattered to the floor sizzled with dark blue ichor that already seemed to be eating holes through the metal.

"I think that's our cue to run again," Alban said. No one argued, but taking flight involved dancing around half a dozen of the spider bots already converging on the toppled shelves, waving their forearms in a good simulation of outrage.

"Take it up with her!" Lark barked at the bots as she thrust an accusing finger back toward the fallen shelves. They were already shuddering again.

The layout of sub-basement six was only slightly convoluted and they made good time across it, but they remained close enough to the stairway down for Sylvie to hear what must have been the protest of the stacked shelves giving way to the persistent battering of the demon. Given how much one simple cardboard box full of books could weigh, that was scarily impressive. That did spark an idea, though. The *Lovelace* movies had made it plain that strengthening a single spell was simpler than maintaining multiple spells. That would be why Lark could levitate a fully loaded bookcase that weighed more than four people but felt she couldn't manage levitating those same four people. "So could you maybe turn a shelf into a flying carpet?" she asked.

A few seconds later, despite Wambleesha's nearly hysterical protests, Lark had an enormous heap of books on the floor and an empty bookshelf hovering in the middle of the main aisle while the others clambered uncomfortably on board. Sylvie held back. "I could see it was hard shifting those full shelves," she said. "I can probably run as fast as you can fly that thing, and you don't need me weighing it down. Move!" Lark nodded her acceptance, and the levitating bookshelf began to accelerate with her standing confidently at the center while all the other riders clung to it for dear life. Sylvie was still keeping pace with only minor effort when it hit the next staircase and shot upward ahead of her, into a sub-basement with actual working lights. That felt great for all of thirty seconds—until Sylvie glanced over her shoulder to spy something arrive at the top of the stair behind them.

The thing was still at least the length of a football field away, only visible because vast galleries dominated the architecture at this level of the archive, so there wasn't much she could make out of its appearance. The most striking things about it at this distance were that it was vaguely humanish, probably naked, structurally female, and entirely colored in various shades of blue, from its long, curved horns and down its bestial legs all the way to its hooves. For one moment Sylvie was surprised they hadn't heard those hooves clattering across the hard floors behind them; then as the thing stepped out into the open gallery and let out another howl, it unfurled its wings and took to the air.

"Bogart at six o'clock!" Sylvie yelled in warning, confusing at least half the people there with her hybrid jargon, but Lark caught her meaning quickly enough and urged more speed out of the flying shelf. By Sylvie's mental calculation, she wasn't sure they'd even be able to make the next stair before the thing caught up with them. Once Alban and Ettie caught sight of the demon they shifted around the back and steadied their small pistols as best they could, holding out for a short-range shot. That was the moment it actually sunk in. That was when Sylvie's stomach dropped with the full understanding that this entire adventure was about to devolve into a brutal close-quarters brawl with a creature that was professionally sadistic, able to bench press at least ten times what she was capable of, and came armed with a nasty-looking set of claws. Worse, it had already shrugged off a blade through the hand as an irritation and...

A montage of movie clips flashed in front of her eyes. "The blood!" She shouted to Alban. "Remember the blood! You can't shoot it point blank!" In fact, the only thing that had saved Ettie earlier was using such a precise, pinpoint weapon against the thing. Any serious gash in its skin could have left her looking like the smoking blade of the broken stiletto. The two locals might not have a library of science fiction movies to fall back on for visual reference, but they winced and nodded, clearly getting her point. Lark glanced back and nodded too. She prepped her riders with a few quick commands.

As expected, the demon was nearly upon them as they approached the next stair. "Now!" Lark shouted. All her passengers hit the floor rolling. Lark and the bookcase came to an abrupt stop then shot upward. The bookcase stopped right in front of the demon's face. Lark kept climbing. The demon hit the solid base of the bookcase head-on and went into a tumbling spin that slammed it into the wall beside the book case. Lark had landed out of sight atop another set of shelves while most of the others took off running back the way they'd come.

Only Alban and Ettie stood their ground while the demon climbed back to its feet, waiting long enough to empty their pistols into its chest in two quick, easy shots each, before turning to flee with the others. The thing screamed, but no one was surprised that it seemed to be more in anger than anything else. It spread its wings to launch itself after its prey again...and Lark dropped the fully loaded bookcase she'd been moving into position above the thing during its precious seconds of recovery. If she'd had just a moment more she might have been able to aim for breaking its neck.

Instead, what the bookshelf hit was one outstretched wing, practically tearing the relatively fragile bones out of their socket and crushing them beneath the enormous weight. Wambleesha screamed as if in agony as she watched ichor spatter across the fallen books, and they instantly burst into flames. While the demon was still trying to wrestle the bookcase off its half-severed wing, Sylvie doubled back and discharged her electroshock wand directly between the thing's shoulder blades. The demon convulsed wildly, then lay still—at least long enough for Lark to drop another bookcase on it.

By this point the archivist had stopped screaming but stood there practically catatonic. Lark swooped back to grab Wambleesha. "Go! Go!" she urged the others. "I've got her." Then they were all scrambling past the heap of books that had already turned into a pyre atop the demon. Sylvie made sure she'd be last in line and was completely ready to leap out of the way when the clawed, blue hand shot out of the pyre in a last moment grab for her ankle.

Narratively, there was no way it couldn't have. The only question was whether it would have led to a narrow escape or the first death. The sigh of relief she'd been intending to let out as she scurried up the stairs turned into more of a sob, but the fact that she wasn't dead right now weighted the odds that this was more action-adventure than horror story. No matter how unstoppable the thing seemed, they *did* have a fighting chance. And the harder they pushed the tropes to conform to adventure over horror, the better she fancied their odds.

It didn't take long for the ear-piercing howls of pursuit to resume, but they were definitely closing the distance more slowly than before. The smashed wing hadn't magically regenerated—another hopeful sign, but people still died in adventure stories. Even if their lives remained locked into narrative rules, too, sometimes tropes got inverted. Arthur Allen had already died in this place. There could be no guarantee that any one of them would live to see the light of day.

The stair up to sub-basement three was still about half a gallery away when Lark suddenly hit the floor and sprawled forward, taking the insensate Wambleesha with her. A moment later the others were there helping them up. Lark looked pale and unsteady. Sylvie would have guessed she'd overextended herself, even without the *Lovelace* movies. Canon in *Lovelace* was that channeling magic power through the body and into spells took a physical toll. Wands existed to take some of the load off, and a good wand could improve the amount of energy an enchanter could channel by several orders of magnitude, but it always caught up with the enchanter eventually. How many tons of books and people had Lark been shifting since they started to run? Apparently the answer was too many.

Alban threw Wambleesha over his shoulders in a fireman's carry, and Sylvie experienced a flicker of gratitude that they'd made it back up as far as they had before Wambleesha had checked out with that glazed look in her eyes. The number of possible wrong turns they could still take had diminished greatly.

Martin started to offer Lark a shoulder to lean on, but she waved him off. "She's after you, not me," Lark said. "Keep moving." Lark wound up leaning on Sylvie with one arm and Brian with the other the rest of the way to the stairs. Ettie relieved Alban of his pistol and took the time to reload both. With a pistol in each hand she began running escort for the group, keeping a nervous eye out for their pursuer. The demon remained out of sight for the moment, but probably around a corner rather than on the level below.

Lark was moving better by the time they got to the top of the stairs. Sylvie left her to Brian and fell back to join Ettie in playing escort. "Honestly," Sylvie asked, "how are we looking here?"

"Honestly honestly?" Ettie asked soberly. "We're losing. With that thing injured, you can get out. Not sure about the rest of us."

Well, by normal rules Sylvie was actually pretty sure they could get six out of seven of them out. All they had to do was abandon Martin. By narrative rules that would backfire even if they were willing to try, but Ettie had seen fit to overlook that option without knowing those rules applied. Sylvie had to respect that.

"Are you up for helping me try something stupid?" Sylvie asked.

"Aren't I already?" Ettie asked.

"Something stupider," Sylvie clarified. Most of the bits inside her skull were already screaming in terror at the plan, but she had to trust to the rules and keep pushing the tropes. No one deep in the heart of an adventure story ever survived by playing it safe.

Even Sylvie was feeling the exertion by the time the stairway up to sub-basement two came in sight. Nearly every gallery on this level was properly lighted, and sightings of the demon behind them were becoming increasingly frequent and distressingly close. It was also becoming clear Lark was about to try to burn energy she didn't have left to burn. At this point she was probably only waiting to see if she could reach the high ground at the top of the stair in time to make use of it again. She'd been moving along at a decent clip again, even if it was on foot, and they couldn't afford to have her cripple herself now.

They rounded a corner. Sylvie split off to take cover between the shelves. Ettie went only a few more paces, then dropped to one knee and readied a pistol. The demon rounded the corner. Ettie's grip held firm on the pistol for one heart beat adjusting her aim, a second heartbeat letting the thing close.

She fired. Once. Twice. The thing shrieked, clutching at its face as blue ichor sprayed around its fingers. Ettie dropped the first pistol, traded the second into her right hand, and pumped two more shots into the demon's exposed stomach. It hurled itself at her in rage, half blind. Ettie had rolled away and was scrambling to her feet a couple of yards to the side. That's when Sylvie hit the thing in the head with a hurled book and charged at it, screaming. Its head whipped around just in time to get hit with a blast of pepper spray. Much to Sylvie's relief, it turned out that demons *did* care about that sort of thing. If she'd dared turn the charge into a running leap, Sylvie might have cleared the blinded demon unscathed, but she feared running into her own cloud of pepper spray and had to fight her own momentum to reverse course instead. She almost made it.

The demon's claws gouged three short but deep lines down her left forearm, sure to leave scars, and her arm exploded with pain. Once she'd scrambled away from the thrashing creature it still took her a moment to realize that even beyond the claw marks, two small drops of ichor had burned holes in her sleeve. The dress had started to smolder, and perhaps the skin beneath it. Someone was screaming—presumably her. She tried to tear off the smoking, blood-soaked sleeve as she stumbled toward the stairs, failed, and began tearing off the entire dress instead. Ettie was there helping her, pulling her away from the blinded demon, then unbuckling the belt and the arm strap that together held what remained of her arsenal so she could finish pulling Sylvie out of the caustic dress. She used the skirts to wipe Sylvie's arm down quickly before tossing the dress aside. Thankfully the shift Sylvie had chosen to line her corset had been sleeveless, so at least she remained clad in those and her petticoats.

Sylvie forced herself to get fully away from the demon and halfway up the stairs before grabbing for the little cork-stoppered vial of colored energy drink she kept sheathed in the arm strap. She emptied it onto the blistering skin of her arm, hoping it would wash away the ichor before it could do any more harm. While she was doing that, Alban rushed past and cracked the blinded demon across the jaw with his cane as it tried to claw its way up the stairs after them. It bought a few more precious seconds for them to reach the top ahead of the thing. Sylvie couldn't be sure past the pain of the claw gouges but she thought she'd succeeded in getting rid of the last traces of ichor. At least the pain had subsided enough for her to want to sob instead of scream.

Brian was wrapping his sling around her arm, trying to staunch the flow of blood. She was feeling lightheaded. "We're going to have matching scars," she heard herself giggle as she tried to help him. His injured arm might be usable but it was still giving him some difficulties.

Then they were off running again. Most of the world drifted out of focus, and Sylvie found herself dividing her willpower between the processes of moving forward and trying not to vomit. It reminded her of the last stages of a marathon but without so much protest from abused legs. Time passed in a fog. There was howling. There was shouting. There were people being pushed and dragged. Then there was a heavy door being slammed, a bolt being thrown. The running stopped. Someone dragged her up one more flight of stairs and settled her into a chair. "First aid kit. On my belt," she heard herself mumbling. Someone was bandaging her arm. It seemed to be a Brian-shaped someone. Sylvie allowed her mind to drift completely out of focus. She slept.

When Sylvie woke, she was stretched out on a couch with her head in Brian's lap while he dozed. She had a kink in her neck, her arm still hurt like blazes, but all seemed quiet and at least two of them were now safely accounted for. "Where are the others?" Sylvie asked.

Brian shook himself fully awake and smiled down at her. "Ettie and Alban are out getting clothes for those of you who need them," he said. "Martin's out cold on the bed. Wambleesha's umm..." He nodded toward a pallet on the floor where the archivist lay with her back to them, facing the fire. Sylvie recognized the fireplace instantly. They were back in the tower, in Lark's rooms. "I'm more worried about her than about Martin. She still hasn't said a word. Wanted her where I could keep an eye on her."

"And Lark?" Sylvie asked.

"Keeping an eye on the door to the sub-basements," he said. "Just in case that thing tries to come through, and to make sure no one tries to go in. Her friends didn't show while we were out, but once they get here the plan is for them to go down together and finish the demon."

"Good," Sylvie murmured, closing her eyes again. Then they shot back open. "It's alive?!"

"Yeah," Brian said. "We weren't exactly in any shape to finish it, even after your crazy stunt."

"And we're just lazing around acting like this is done?!" she asked in alarm. "That's not how this works!"

"Lark's got this," he assured her. "She'll come let us know if it starts battering at the door."

Sylvie struggled to sit up and wound up rolling off the couch, onto her knees. "It doesn't have to come through the door, Brian! It can get out with the bots!"

"What?!" he asked in alarm.

"Those crawlers hauling out rock from the mining," she said. "Where do you think all that rock was going? It's not getting hauled out through the front door of the library. There's a back exit!" She scrambled to her feet and rushed out the door to peer down the central shaft of the tower. Brian scrambled after her. There wasn't much to see. To call the shaft dimly lit would have been charitable.

"Whatcha think?" Brian asked. "Is it down there?"

"Coin toss," Sylvie sighed, then hurried up the stairs to the belfry. Again he followed her. A glow off through the fog hinted that it was still early in the morning. At least the fog didn't seem quite so thick. "Keep an eye on the stair," she told him as she skirted around the belfry, checking each side as she peered over the outer edges. "No...no...no...Go!" she shouted, nearly pushing him down the stairs in her haste.

"Any time?" Brian demanded.

"Maybe a minute?" Sylvie guessed. "It's still a ways down, but I don't know how fast it can climb."

Brian burst back into Lark's sitting room and tried to shake Wambleesha out of her daze. Still nothing. "I've got her," he said, trying awkwardly to lift the woman onto his shoulders. "You wake Martin."

"Isn't the stair out?!" Sylvie asked. "Lark said the stair was out!"

"The stair is out," Brian confirmed, horror dawning on his face along with the memory. "We can't get out, but you can. Go! Get Lark. The door's mostly steel. It's got a bar. We can hold out until—"

"Is she even recovered?" Sylvie demanded.

"Of course she—"

"Is she recovered?!" Sylvie glared.

Biting his lip, Brian shook his head silently.

She grabbed the heavy outer door. He joined her. Together they pulled and pulled until it thudded closed. They slammed the bar down to secure it in place. Then Sylvie turned to Brian and kissed him soundly. "Thanks for trying," she said. "Don't ever try to trick me into letting you play martyr again." She scrambled for the phone and began trying Lark's friends. "Amy?" she tried. "Holly? Isaac?" When they all met with dead air she even tried Eli, though she doubted he could be anywhere near a phone. "Dammit!" she slammed down the receiver. As if in echo, a hammering started at the door. "Keep trying to wake her up," Sylvie said, gesturing to Wambleesha. "Maybe she can get calls through that we can't." Remembering her one successful call from the phone, Sylvie picked up the receiver again. "Nami, please," she said, forcing herself to maintain a veneer of calm as she waited for an answer.

"Hello?" Nami's voice answered, unmistakably puzzled.

"Nami! Yes! Where are you?" Sylvie asked.

"On the train back. Target sedated, mission accomplished. Are you all right? How did you even—"

"No time! Can you get to the cathedral, like, quick? We're in trouble."

"Let me put you on speaker," she said.

"Sylvie! Sorry we missed you," Diana said. "Something's wrong?"

"Just in a panic room in the highest belfry of the cathedral with a demon pounding on the door so she can get in and kill Martin," Sylvie said in a rush.

"Martin's safe," Diana said, confused. "We've got him right here."

"You've got Eli! *We've* got Martin. Brian's trapped here with me. And an innocent archivist."

"Can you hold out for an hour?" Diana asked.

"I doubt it," Sylvie said. "She's *really* strong."

"Okay. I'll put Felicity on figuring out the rituals to deal with this while I figure out how to get us there faster," Diana said. "Do whatever you can to buy us time."

"We need another plan," Sylvie sighed miserably as she hung up. "The way those hinges are rattling I don't think we have fifteen minutes."

"Well, we're surrounded by fictional characters," Brian said. "Got the number for Cyn and Scott Legacy?" he asked, nodding toward the phone.

Sylvie smiled ruefully. "Doesn't work that way. Lark uses it to talk to her friends, but I can only seem to get people from...back...home..."

"Lenore?" Brian asked.

Sylvie nodded vigorously and picked up the phone again. It went straight to voice mail. She slammed down the receiver and tried again.

"Hello?" a woman's voice answered groggily.

"Lenore?! It's Sylvie!"

"This is an emergency?" Lenore asked. "I've got a social psyche test this afternoon and..."

"Big emergency!" Sylvie assured her. "Dark Legacy trivia contest! I need an expert like *now*."

"I'm in," Lenore said. "What's the question? And what's that pounding?"

"Count-down timer."

"And the screeching?"

"Atmosphere. Building the pressure. First, you remember that episode with Cyn and Scott trapped in the penthouse?"

Lenore snorted. "*The Fallen Shall Rise*? Sure."

"There was a ritual. A banishment chant they used to get rid of the demons, right?" Sylvie asked.

"Yeah. They never gave it a name in the show, though. Fans call it—"

"I don't need the name," Sylvie said hastily. "I need the chant. The exact chant. The whole thing. Syllable for syllable. Do you know where—"

It was Lenore's turn to interrupt. "You mean, '*Nisl nisi scelerisque eu ultrices vitae auctor eu augue*,' and so on?"

"Yes! Brian, where's my belt? Get a pen and the pad I was using to map."

"You know this is a ridiculous long shot?" he asked as he handed them to her. "It's just a silly chant out of a show."

"And we're just in a book," Sylvie said, covering the mouthpiece. "And that thing out there came out of *another* book. It's fiction all the way down."

"Lenore, you're a life saver," Sylvie said into the phone. "Now they used candles, too, didn't they? Eighteen? That's a lot of candles. Yeah, I know you didn't design the set. What else? Bells? Did you get that, Brian? Candles and bells."

"No book?" he asked.

"Only for the incantation," Sylvie said as Brian scrambled around, ransacking Lark's rooms.

The top hinge of the door was starting to tear free when Brian returned from the interior rooms.

"Six candles?! That's it?! No bell?!" Sylvie asked in alarm.

"I've got it! I've got it!" Brian insisted, scrabbling through her tool belt until he came up with a pocketknife. He laid the candles out side by side on the floor and sliced through them rapidly. With each candle in three parts he scooped them all into a pillow case and tossed it to her. "You've got a lighter, right?" he asked. "I didn't see it."

"Yeah!" She skidded up to the belt on her knees scanned its length, looking for the lighter. "The bells?"

"On it. You set up the candles." He pulled out his phone and started tapping at the interface.

The top hinge on the door screamed as it tore free from the frame. The snarling face of the demon appeared in the gap. Sylvie kept lighting candles as quickly as her shaking hands would allow. Eleven. Twelve. Thirteen...The door came crashing down with a force that shook the entire room and fractured floorboards. Sylvie heard herself whimper as one of the candles went out and she had to relight it. Sixteen. Seventeen. The demon's ear-piercing howl filled the world. Eighteen!

Sylvie spun to face the thing without getting off her knees, held up the phonetic transcription of the chant, and began to read at the same time that Brian held up his phone, blasting its little speakers at full volume with the merry sound of sleigh bells. Sylvie refused to let it give her pause. "*Nisl nisi scelerisque eu ultrice,*" she recited loudly. The demon stopped and stared down at her, wide eyed, as the snarl vanished from its face. Was it working? She couldn't believe this hastily cobbled together plan was working. She forced the nonsense words to keep coming while the demon stood accommodatingly frozen.

"*Vel fringilla est ullamcorper eget nulla facilisi etiam dignissim diam. Ullamcorper dignissim cras tincidunt lobortis,*" she finished at last. A light breeze stirred the flames of the candles. A pained expression flickered across the demon's face, to be replaced with one of rage. It stepped forward with another howl that echoed deafeningly through the small room. Before Sylvie could even get off her knees, the demon had her by the throat and was lifting her in the air, its claws biting painfully into her flesh.

Brian came rushing in, swinging the iron poker from the fireplace. It struck the demon's shoulder about where its tattered wing must have connected. It howled in pain, but its grip on Sylvie's throat only tightened cruelly while its other hand sent Brian flying over the couch with a backhand swat. It lowered Sylvie to inches in front of its face. If she wasn't already choking she would have gagged on its noxious breath as it looked her in the eye and snarled, "*Ullamcorper* dignissit *cras tincidunt lobortis. Dignissit! Dignissit!* Not *dignissim*. Start over. Get it right." It tossed her roughly back to the floor and stood, waiting expectantly. When she hesitated, it snarled.

"Ummm...*Nisl nisi scelerisque eu ultrice,*" Sylvie began again hesitantly, remembering the admonition that when arcane magic makes random things happen, they're almost always bad. What did this creature know that she didn't? What was she on the verge of unleashing? She could still stop. It would probably cost her life, but she could still stop. Her voice faltered and trailed off. The demon snarled and hissed, flexing its claws as it stepped toward her again. Then Brian reappeared, sliding between her and the demon, his arms up defensively, his hands open placatingly.

"She'll do it!" he said in a rush. "We'll do it!"

"Start...again," the demon hissed.

Brian turned to Sylvie, holding out his hand for the notepad. "You want me to do it?"

"You promised!" she said accusingly, fighting to hold back the tears.

"I'm not playing martyr," he said, clearly working hard to maintain control himself. "It's going to be all right. *She just wants to go home.*"

Sylvie looked up past Brian at the demon. It had calmed again, and it gave the barest hint of what could be a nod as she met its disconcerting gaze.

"I've got this," Sylvie said to Brian, her voice barely coming out as a whisper. She cleared her throat and began again. "*Nisl nisi scelerisque eu ultrice...*" Her voice kept trying to break. The notepad trembled in her hand. Right up until the very last syllable fell from her lips a part of her head was screaming that Brian had it all wrong, that cruel deceit was what demons did, and that this was the part of the movie where the trusting dupe opened up the portal to unleash all the forces of hell on an unsuspecting world. But when the hellscape shimmered into existence behind the demon it simply seemed to wrap her in a welcoming embrace. The creature threw up her hands and threw back her head as in ecstatic release, then demon and portal were gone, leaving behind nothing more than a noxious hint of sulfur in the air.

Every awareness of danger, every rush of emotion Sylvie had been suppressing just to keep moving came for her at once and she found herself curled up halfway into a ball, sobbing uncontrollably until she was gasping for air. At some point she realized Brian was holding her, rocking her, saying nothing. He might be on the edge of a breakdown too, but if he was, she'd beat him to the punch, and he'd managed to keep deferring it for her sake. "Okay. Okay," she sobbed when her lungs had managed to re-inflate a bit. "You passed the roller coaster test." She kissed him. He kissed her back. They were small kisses, messy kisses, full of more tears than passion, but they were real, and they were undeniably right.

"Not just going to give me an exemption?" he chuckled softly. She could see his face now and confirm he was a mess too.

"No exemption," she agreed, trying to wipe the tears off her cheeks. "I'm rewriting the whole damn test."

He smiled. She smiled back. He cocked his head. "Did you...hear that?" he asked.

Listening through a renewed grip of apprehension, she finally heard it too and let out a held breath. "I never hung up on Lenore!" Sylvie scrambled to the telephone, never quite making it to her feet until she had the fireplace to lean on. "Yes! Yes! Everything's all right! You were beyond great. Okay, no I can't explain all that stuff right now. I will. I swear if you'll swear too. Big huge secret stuff. Yes, soon! I *have* to make another call. I owe you!"

Sylvie hung up the phone, picked it up again and was about to ask for Nami when Martin Kight, wrapped in a quilt, poked his head cautiously out from the inner door. "Is she gone?" he asked.

CHAPTER TEN
WAKING UP

"I didn't even get to say goodbye!" Sylvie wailed.

"You'll get your chance," Diana assured her over the phone. "We needed to get Eli home ASAP, and some of the others were barely holding it together. We'll keep their bridge open, though, and fly you out here as soon as you're packed. We owe them help getting their lives sorted out, and right now that's all on Kassia. No one needs me or Felicity poking around Lovelace right now."

"Okay. Yeah," Sylvie said, mollified. She and Brian had been busy trying to take care of Wambleesha when the decision had been made very abruptly to hustle the *Lovelace* crew off home by way of I-15. To be fair to the senior Freyjur about that decision, Eli had become no less unhinged than when they thought he was Martin and had held them at gunpoint. Plus, his sister, Amy, was on the verge of violence herself over getting him home safe and without delay.

No one wanted to even try getting them all through the airport, and it had been quickly agreed that they should recreate the conditions of the original bridge as closely as possible, changing only those variables that they absolutely had to. Accidentally dropping them into a world sort of like the one they'd come from, but not actually it, would have turned into a nightmare. The original bridge had been opened back in L.A.—where they could also find Sonja McMullin, who had participated in the original ritual—so off they'd gone, leaving only Manami behind with the hotel room keys to help Sylvie sort things out here. Neither of them had been there the first time, so replacing them with members of the *Lovelace* crew hadn't left the outcome of the spell any more problematic.

"How is your archivist friend doing?" Diana asked.

"Better. Some," Sylvie said. "Alban's good with her, what with his unfair insights into people. He says there really is some sort of psychic connection between her and the archive, that it's more than emotional trauma, but we're optimistic."

When the call was over, Sylvie came out of the bedroom to find Brian in the main room of the suite, his books and papers from his day of coursework spread out on the coffee table in front of him. For a few seconds he remained lost in the paper he was staring at while he chewed at the tip of a pencil—a practical case study in scholarly stereotype that his Victorian-style waistcoat and pocket watch only reinforced. Finally laying the paper aside he looked up and smiled at her. "Are you ready?"

"You tell me," she said, her skirts fanning out as she twirled for him. The dress was a compromise between the flirty costume she'd worn for the convention and the conservative dress she'd worn to the cathedral. Sleeveless and off-the shoulder, the long black dress remained businesslike in all the other particulars. She'd even opted to leave off her arsenal this time with all its accompanying leather. In a nod to whimsy, though, she'd added the bowler hat from her original costume, complete with Nami's plush dragon.

"Well, I like the short skirts, but yeah. This is beautiful too," he said. "Very elegant."

"Thank you," she said, allowing herself to bask in the simple warmth of the compliment in a way she wouldn't have a week ago. The cravings had always left her feeling a little bit frivolous before. It was clear now they were just a part of who she was. She could live with that and try not to beat herself up over it. And of course, a week ago she wouldn't have let herself think of the compliment as anything more than a cordial observation coming from Brian. "Elegant seemed a lot more appropriate for a wake. I got a text from Nami. She's running a bit late. I told her we'd wait for her down at the front door."

Giving a nod, Brian started gathering his scattered papers into a neat pile on the corner of the table, then got up and pulled on his coat. Sylvie scooped up the top hat he'd left on the side table and plopped it on his head while he was still buttoning the coat. They exchanged grins while he finished, then she grabbed him by the lapels and pulled him into a leisurely kiss.

"Oh. Hey. Sorry. I think I missed something," Lenore said, emerging from the bathroom. "Okay, I missed a lot of stuff, but I didn't know I'd missed that one yet. Did you finally get him on that roller coaster?"

"Yeah." Sylvie smiled at Lenore, releasing Brian from the kiss without releasing his lapels. "It was a wild ride. You look good."

"Thanks." Getting Lenore into black was out of the question, no matter the occasion. Like everything else about the self-proclaimed Goth princess, her Victorianish outfit was thoroughly pink. She had already informed them that it was not a steampunk costume but a loaner that the UNLV had last used in a production of "Hello Dolly"—still not quite Victorian but closer to the real thing than steampunk was. Lenore didn't do the full turn for them, but did swish the skirts a bit. "Did I hear that Nami's going to be late?"

"A bit. Don't worry. We can go ahead and break the suspense," Sylvie said, gesturing toward the door into Teprigoth.

"I'm still coming to grips with you being in some sort of club with Diana Taylor and Felicity Ward," Lenore said. "I can't imagine what you're still keeping from..." She peered through the now-open door. "The big secret isn't just remodeling, is it?"

Sylvie shook her head and chuckled, shooing Lenore on in.

"Oh, my," Lenore said, stepping out onto the landing. "This can't..." Her voice trailed off as her delighted eyes took in the haunted atmosphere.

"No," Brian assured her. "It can't. Come on." He led the way on down the stairs to where a small, spotted cat sat patiently, twitching its tail.

"You must be Lenore," Loki said cordially. "As the founding member of the Freyjur Auxiliary, I welcome you to the team and look forward to working with you closely."

Lenore's mouth dropped open. "Yes," Sylvie said, gently closing it for her. "The cat did just talk. His name is Loki."

Lenore took a couple more seconds, allowing that to process, then asked, "Team?"

"Should I make the joke about the cat being out of the bag," Brian asked, "or just let that one go?"

"Let it go," Loki sighed. "It will be better for everyone."

"Technically not yet. I mean, Lark will want to extend the offer herself, but after we told them what you did and vouched for you, they practically begged for you to come join. You've got the mad skillz, girl."

"It's a *Dark Legacy* club?!" Lenore asked excitedly.

"Not exactly," Sylvie said, producing a small jewelry bag and pouring out a pair of rings into Lenore's hand. "Put these on and we'll fill you in."

An hour later, the four of them were sitting together with Manami in a carriage at the end of a small, somber procession as it clattered across the dark plaza and through the gates of Poppikin Park. At the hands of a robotic footman, the iron grillwork swung slowly closed behind them, followed by an inner pair of solid wooden gates, leaving the procession alone in the park with only the low-lying electric lights along the pathways to mark the way through fog-shrouded night.

"So, you basically saved four lives," Sylvie said as they carried on through the silent park. "You contributed a brand-new ritual. You walked me through my first spell. You helped break ground for a whole new field of research, adapting what should be fictional nonsense into effective magic. And your ability to absorb and memorize all this stuff phonetically? We've got nothing like that, and it makes you a natural for working with the rituals. All that plus character witnesses? They'd be crazy if they *didn't* want you."

Lenore beamed. "And there's no dress code?"

"You would *not* have to wear black. Or much of anything else, I guess," Nami said, unable to stifle a laugh. Even Lenore smirked. They'd already covered the basics of *la química*. "But, yeah, no one's going to stifle your fashion sense."

"Looks like we're here," Brian said as the carriage slowed to a stop near the entrance to the canal tour. Loki hopped up onto Brian's shoulder as they climbed out, and he rode there as they walked over to join the others. The two seemed to have bonded quickly. The fact that Brian seemed content with the thought of *not* studying magic himself as long as he could come along for the rides might have had something to do with it. It meant that Loki was no longer alone in playing a supporting role to the real magicians, and he clearly relished his position as the senior member of that little fraternity. Sylvie had been a little surprised to find Brian wasn't falling over himself to learn magic, but he'd said that he already had way too many arcane rituals to master if he was going to have any hope of passing the bar.

Alban, Ettie, and Wambleesha were waiting for them by the edge of the canal. Wambleesha still looked dazed and detached, but it was a marked improvement over the glassy-eyed stare that had spent nearly three days on her face. When Loki hopped from Brian's shoulder over to hers she accepted it, even acknowledging him by stroking his ears. Then the carriage drivers—who'd been introduced as colleagues of Alban and Ettie—climbed down and went about unloading the casket from the hearse. They lowered into the old barge that had been moored at the dock, then opened it and stepped away.

"Tonight we gather in memory of those who made the ultimate sacrifice so that we might live," Alban said, assuming a place at the edge of the dock. "Precious few tragedies can compare with the loss of knowledge, for when knowledge dies a little part of us dies with it. There is no trivial fact any more than there is a trivial life. Facts are the sum and summary of who we are, who we were, and the potentials of our future. Who can say that what goes unrecognized, unacknowledged, unrecorded ever really happened at all?"

One of the carriage drivers lit a torch and passed it to Alban. Alban offered it to Wambleesha, who accepted it, teary-eyed. Then she stepped up and tossed the torch into the casket. As the mooring was released, the collected unsalvageable books that they'd hauled up from the archives caught fire. The barge was pushed away from the docks and drifted slowly away, a Viking funeral set to an old Irish dirge courtesy of Brian's phone. The carriage drivers quietly withdrew and headed for the service entrance to the canal tour, where they'd have to deal with the mess. The tour canal wasn't really designed to submerge a boat in but everyone neglected to point that out to Wambleesha. Funerals were for the sake of the living. It did seem to bring some color back to her cheeks and some focus to her eyes.

Soon after the barge had disappeared around the first bend in the tunnel, the lights and music of the carousel started up in the distance, a beacon in the fog that called their little gathering in. "Did you get a chance to try Lark's phone today?" Brian asked as he and Sylvie strolled together toward the carousel.

"Yeah," Sylvie said. "It's dead. Diana and Felicity will probably be disappointed. I'm not. It wasn't working like *anyone* expected. Continuing to use it might be playing with fire." Also, the secret of talking to Arthur was one she was pleased to have no reason to agonize over keeping. He'd accomplished what he wanted and had gotten Martin to safety. Or maybe the cathedral had done that by pretending to be him. Anyway, the hope of talking to the dead was notorious for driving people to do foolish things. If the phone no longer worked at all, telling Diana and Felicity about talking to Arthur would just be pointless cruelty—and she could go through her life pretending it had never happened.

"Martin sends his apologies for not being here," Sylvie said to Wambleesha as the gathering reconvened at the carousel. "He's in a hospital now, under observation, but he'd have never made it home at all if not for your help." Wambleesha gave a little nod of acceptance, biting her lip.

Perched on a nearby bench, Ettie pulled a wine bottle out of a small crate that had been left there and used the accompanying corkscrew to deftly open it. "All right," she said, rising. "The sad bit's over. Now we ride carousels, drink like barbarians, and celebrate the existence of good books." She stood, tipped her head back, and poured a generous swallow from the bottle straight into her open mouth. Ignoring the fact that at least a quarter of it actually spattered over her chin and down her bodice, she met Wambleesha's eyes with a savage grin and thrust the bottle at her. "To cheap novels, dry public ledgers, and intimate personal journals. Without them, would we even know who we are?"

Wambleesha accepted the bottle and the toast with a tentative smile, but then only stared dubiously at the bottle.

"Do you drink?" Ettie asked her.

"Sometimes," Wambleesha said quietly.

"Can you think of some time that's better than now?" Ettie asked.

Wambleesha continued to stare at the bottle for a couple more seconds before whispering, "Books." She lifted the bottle a bit, lowered it, then tried again. "Books," she repeated. This time there was a little strength to her voice. She raised the bottle to her lips and took a healthy swallow. She coughed and spluttered, spitting half of it out on the ground. It seemed to have started down the wrong way, but Wambleesha waved away any hint of assistance while she coughed for a bit; then she raised the bottle and tried again. This try came off much better. When she'd swallowed, she repeated one more time, "Books."

"Books," the others agreed, raising the bottles Alban had been passing around. The range of alcohols with a taste Sylvie cared for was pretty narrow, and although wine wasn't among them she could put up with it for the sake of the occasion. She also hoped that simply joining in drinking straight from the bottle counted as barbaric enough. She was feeling too subdued to get into the idea of spilling it carelessly. Wasn't that the point of a wake, though, to cast off that emotional weight? Maybe. She'd always heard about them, but this was the first gathering she'd attended that called itself one.

She lost herself briefly in thought. When she came back to the world, Wambleesha was allowing Alban to boost her up onto a carousel horse, where she perched side-saddle with one hand gripping the bar and the other hand gripping the bottle. The self-conscious, uncertain look on her face would have made Sylvie uncomfortable for her if not for the fact it was the most engaged she'd looked since they'd returned to the surface. Ettie climbed up onto a horse beside the archivist, still clutching a bottle of her own, and Alban waved the rest of the gathering to join them as he retreated to the controls. In a move that would have made the lawyers at an earthly amusement park cringe, he started the carousel moving before hopping lightly aboard himself and joining them.

To a girl addicted to twenty-first-century thrill rides, the motion of the carousel was mild to say the least, with nothing but those unusual hills to add any real interest. That didn't dampen her appreciation for the fact it was on another world, or make its calliope tune any less lively. Sylvie found no small contentment in sedately clinging to the horse and exchanging smiles with Brian, who'd wound up sitting on the horse beside her. More than once, though, as they glided over the hills of the carousel, she caught him watching Ettie, and about the fifth time around he caught her catching him and his smile turned apologetic. Sylvie waved a hand dismissively and leaned across the gap between them to say quietly, "I'm not going anywhere, but you'll probably never see her again after tonight."

"You're *really* okay with it?" he asked. "I know—"

"Yes. I am," she cut him off firmly. She'd better be. That particular fairy story had set sail. Let someone else be the princess with the happily ever after. She had her heart set on playing the wicked enchantress—or at least on playing the naughty one.

"I know you know this one," Ettie was saying to Wambleesha.

"Which one?" Wambleesha asked, finally stringing two whole words together into a sentence.

"This one," Ettie repeated, inclining her head toward the carousel's mirrored central pillar. "What's the song's name?"

"Evergreen?" Wambleesha said.

"Right!" Ettie said, striking herself a gentle blow to the forehead with the heel of her palm. "'The Land of Evergreen'."

She began *da-da-dumming* along with the calliope for several bars before breaking into a song fit for an old music hall. She had a nice voice for it.

Then the Lady said, 'What?"
And the Gent said, 'Where?"
And a wink passed in-between.
Then the little black cat in the pink top hat
Said, "Come along with me.
With a trill-a-rill-a-ray we will find our way
to the Land of Evergreen.
With a trill-a-rill-a-ray we will find our way
to the Land of Evergreen."

Alban joined her after that, and the song turned out to have a surprising amount of innuendo for a Victorianish carousel tune. Maybe the carousel had a special "after dark" playlist, or maybe this was just one of those songs with a million verses made up by tavern-goers. In any event, Sylvie, Brian, Nami, and Lenore all found themselves drafted into singing along with the chorus after a few verses. Within a few minutes even Wambleesha could be heard *trill-a-rill-a-raying* along and each rider on the carousel was clutching a bottle of wine that no one could have mistaken for full.

Twice the tune switched, and twice Alban and Ettie led them in a new song before Alban finally dismounted and brought the ride to a stop. From there they adjourned to the carnival games, where Alban kept putting a ball back into Wambleesha's hand until she'd managed to knock over an entire pyramid of bottles. Disappointingly there were no plush animals waiting to force on her; just a collection of cheap plaster sculptures. No one volunteered that as a good idea under the circumstance, so they simply moved on again to the nearby fun house. When its lights came on it did indeed transform from eerie to inviting. Halfway through a black-light maze full of glowing psychedelic designs that would have been totally anachronistic in the real Victorian era, Sylvie found herself making out in a dark dead-end with Alban while the sounds of their companions faded in the distance.

"Thank you," she murmured during their first intermission. "For this. The wake. I was feeling so guilty for getting her into that mess."

"Don't. She's going to be all right. And Wambleesha's a big girl," Alban assured her, "no matter how child-like she can seem. If any of us knew the risks, it was her."

The next time they came up for air, he already had her half out of her dress and she was eagerly helping him. "So what's your thinking on that roller-coaster ride?" he asked breathlessly.

ꙮ

It wasn't until the bridge had closed behind Sylvie and she was halfway to L.A., with Nami taking her shift at the wheel of their rental moving van, that she realized they'd never made it to that roller coaster. She didn't let that get her down, though. She just sighed, closed her eyes, and played back the time she'd spent playing hide-and-seek with Alban through the fun-house mirror maze, more than half hoping all the while that Brian would come looking for her before she managed to find her way back to her clothes. His loss.

When they arrived in L.A. they parked the truck outside Felicity's modest mansion and left it loaded pending the final decision on a destination for their furniture. Between online searches and the help of Felicity's favorite real estate agent they'd pulled together a handful of reasonable options. Leaving the bridge unattended until it was closed, though, had been out of the question, so tomorrow would be for checking them out and hopefully signing some paperwork. The following Monday they both had job interviews. Brian had promised he'd be joining them, but it would be weeks yet before his loose ends got tied up and his arrangements and final plans solidified. Neither Sylvie nor Nami had any doubt they'd be seeing Lenore out here as well. Nothing had been finalized there, but the leaders of the coven could be so very persuasive and magic so seductive. The matter was entirely a question of when, not if.

Felicity wasn't home, but she'd given them the code to the guest house out by the pool. They let themselves in, each claimed one of the two available beds, then ordered take-out and unpacked their overnight bags. Nami slipped into a bikini and insisted Sylvie play poolside photographer so she could update her social media pages with news of her grand arrival in Hollywood. There didn't seem to be any streaming service on the guest-house television, but they lucked into catching the start of *Interstellar: Risen Heretics*, the second movie of the recently rebooted franchise.

Sylvie fell asleep watching it with her head in Nami's lap before their dinner had even arrived. She woke alone on the couch with the bright morning sun streaming in the windows and *Learning to Spell*, the first of the *Lovelace* movies, playing on the television. Diana was curled up in the nearby recliner, watching it.

"I guess you're not one of those actors who hates watching herself," Sylvie said, pulling herself up sleepily.

Diana flashed her a smile. "Creepy seeing this all happen in the third person. Creepier that if any of the details are wrong, I can't spot them."

Sylvie's eyes widened at the sound of the American accent. "Lark? I thought you went home."

"Been there. Done that," Lark said. "Feeling quite a bit better, thanks."

Before she knew what she was doing, Sylvie was off the couching and hugging the woman fiercely while Lark patted her reassuringly on the shoulder.

"Didn't think I was just going to disappear on you after all that, did you?" Lark asked. "They left the bridge open for me. It'll even be good for a few more days." She managed to fumble with the remote until she got the movie paused, then—after one final squeeze—managed to get up and shift their conversation over to the couch.

Sylvie found her eyes were clouding up and she wiped them clear with the back of her hand. "I've only spent about half my life waiting for that adventure," she said. "And I know this is stupid—and, yeah, creepy—but for a lot of that time you were my best friend in the world."

"No. I get it," Lark said with a gentle smile. "I've got my imaginary friends, too. And apparently, they're out there somewhere every bit as real. Did you grow up hearing about the infinite number of monkeys banging out a script for 'Hamlet' or was that just in my world? Anyway, I guess you get the same sort of genius out of an infinite number of molecules. You're pretty amazing, you know. I can live with you being the best friend I never had."

The tears stopped being mere blurs at the edge of Sylvie's vision. When she'd recovered enough to see straight, she found Lark holding out a long, slender box to her. "Sylvie, you gave me my life back. You gave all of us our lives back. I know you didn't open the bridge, but you believed in me, and you came looking for me when no one else would have. Without you the bridge would have closed without us finding it, and without your friends even dreaming we were there. So 'goodbye' isn't enough. Even 'thank you' is barely a start."

Sylvie accepted the box with some trepidation. She'd gone through this whole gifting train of thought with Wambleesha, trying to think of some small way to make amends, and realized how hard it was to come up with a personally meaningful gift for her that wouldn't just be dust within the month. She braced herself now as she opened the box, to simply appreciate the thought. She was glad she had. There in the box lay Lark's own wand, exactly like she'd seen it in the movies, with its marbled blue handle and its tapered, silvery shaft covered in scrollwork designs. Even braced as she was, Sylvie's breath caught in her throat for several seconds, then she found herself stammering, "Oh, Lark. I...I can't..."

"You can," Lark assured her. "It's not going to vanish on you. It's not mine—just a replica made right here in your world. Your friends helped me arrange a little keepsake for you."

Sylvie couldn't stop crying, but she smiled past the tears. "Does it...Does it work?"

"Funny you should ask," Lark grinned. "*I* can make it do things. You? Not a clue. I figured we could find out together."

Other Titles in the
FREYJUR FANTASIES

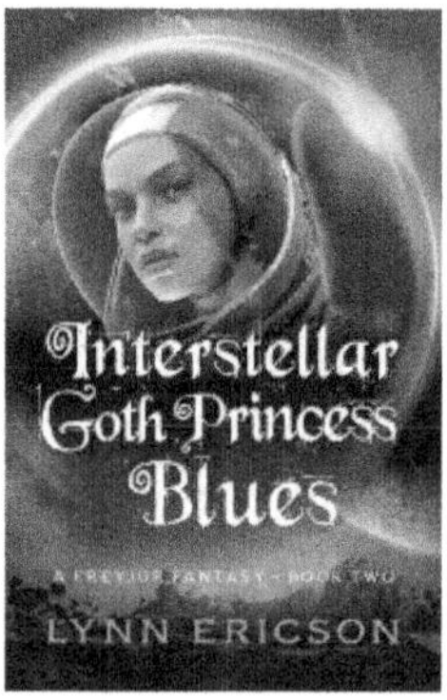

Book Two
INTERSTELLAR GOTH PRINCESS BLUES

978-1-956243-02-4

A Universe of Trouble

As a modern coven of urban witches, the Freyjur step into works of fiction for fun and profit.

Arguably the most fun part is la química, a heady sexual chemistry that suffuses every world they step into regardless of the original fiction.

But Lenore isn't a bit comfortable with the hedonistic flings that come with the territory. She dreads the emotional investment of getting caught up in a whirlwind romance that's all too quickly over.

So when the coven ventures into the sprawling, space-opera universe of Space Jockey Zero, it's all a business trip for Lenore. She's there to cure cancer, nothing else.

Then a case of mistaken identity leaves her stranded and alone.

To linger in the alien reality can bring only madness—but before Lenore can hope to get home she'll have to stop an interstellar war, teach the greatest threat to galactic civilization how to be evil, and find some way to deal with a whirlwind romance that's going terribly right.

At least there's cocoa.